EPISODE ON THE RIVIERA

ALSO BY MACK REYNOLDS

Ability Quotient
After Some Tomorrow
After Utopia
Amazon Planet
Black Man's Burden
Border, Breed nor Birth
Brain World
Code Duello
Commune 2000AD
Computer War
Computer World
Dawnman Planet
Day After Tomorrow
Depression or Bust
Equality in the Year 2000
Galactic Medal of Honour
Lagrange Five
Looking Backward from the Year 2000
Mercenary from Tomorrow
Of Godlike Power (aka Earth Unaware)
Perchance to Dream
Planetary Agent X
Police Patrol: 2000AD
Rolltown
Satellite City
Section G: United Planets
Space Pioneer
Space Search
Space Visitor
The Best Ye Breed
The Computer Conspiracy
The Cosmic Eye
The Earth War
The Five-way Secret Agent
The Fracas Factor
The Rival Rigelians
The Space Barbarians
The Towers of Utopia
Time Gladiator
Tomorrow Might be Different
Trample an Empire Down

EPISODE ON THE RIVIERA

MACK REYNOLDS

WILDSIDE PRESS

CHAPTER ONE

Friday, August 5th

Steven Philip Cogswell awakened and grunted discomfort. He opened one eye experimentally, then closed it again. On the pillow next to his was a blond head. He forced himself to think back.

The party last night at the contessa's. But a blonde? What blonde? As he recalled, he'd started the evening with a petite brunette up from Cannes. He tried to remember the blondes who had been present. Maggie Fontaine, Betty Smith-Browne, and that German baroness or whatever she was. But none of them had been *this* blond.

He opened his eyes again, both of them this time. Holy smokes, it was Conny's girl friend! The Greek was going to be sore as a slipped disc. Steve looked at her distastefully, which was characteristic enough. He couldn't bear the sight of a girl the morning afterward. What had ever gotten into him!

Constantine Kamiros was a long-time friend and he'd been hot after this wench. It was a dirty trick to pull on the Greek, especially since Steve Cogswell couldn't have cared less. A blonde was just one more blonde on the Côte d'Azur in season.

There was probably no stretch of shoreline in the world with more feminine pulchritude per square foot than that lying between Marseille at one end and Menton, on the Italian border, at the other.

On top of everything else, the girl was one of Steve's clients, one of the Far Away Holiday tourists down from London on the luxury package holiday. This was her second week on the Riviera. Conny had talked her into extending her stay. *Talked* her was a gentle way of putting it. The Greek gambler and shipping magnate had been lavishing presents on the girl as though he meant to marry her.

Steve pursed his lips unhappily, trying to remember what had happened. As was usual at one of Carla Rossi's parties, he'd gotten well stoned. It came back to him now.

He'd been drinking French Seventy-fives. What was the formula? One jigger of dry gin, one-third jigger of lemon juice, one teaspoon of powdered sugar; pour into a tall glass one-half full of cracked ice and fill with chilled Champagne. They were bad enough but he hadn't the good sense to stick to them. Dave Shepherd, that fluttery limp-wrist had come up with a bottle of absinthe he'd smuggled in from his last trip to Tangiers and they'd all had to try it. The illegal green liqueur, complete with its wormwood base, had tasted like ordinary Pernod—but it hadn't the same effect.

What was the wise crack Dave had made? *Absinthe makes the heart grow fonder*. Well, he was right. The stuff was an aphrodisiac if there ever was one.

Steve looked at the girl again. Her back was to him, her hair spilled disorderly over the whiteness of the pillow, one arm outside the sheet and the greater part of one rounded breast proudly exposing itself. She was obviously nude beneath the bedclothes. The Greek had good taste, Steve Cogswell decided sourly. The girl was lushly beautiful.

It was still early. Steve could tell that from the light that streamed in the window of his house trailer—caravans, they called them over here. He shifted quietly, not wanting to wake her. Just as sure as certainty, if she awoke she'd expect a repetition of last night's erotic activity, and, frankly, Steve Cogswell wasn't up to it.

He was no more up to love-making in the morning than he was up to early morning drinking. He couldn't stand the sight of the stuff, and he meant that both ways. He could have spurned a composite of Cleopatra and Helen of Troy—the morning after.

Why not face it? he told himself glumly. It wasn't just the fact that it was morning. He couldn't stand the sight of a women—any woman—once he'd bedded her. The very thought of a repeat performance, the following day or the following week, was all the same. He simply couldn't bear the sight of them.

He wondered if his smoking a cigarette would awaken her. He just couldn't lie here motionless. In half an hour he'd have an excuse for deserting her; he'd have to round up his tourists and get them ready for the return flight to London.

His cigarettes were in the little stand at the head of the bed. There were two packs, one of Camels, one of the local Gauloise. He loathed the French brand, but his supply of American cigarettes was running distressingly low.

He'd have to talk one of the sailors over at Villefranche, the Sixth Fleet base, out of another carton, which was highly illegal, of course. But American cigarettes in France, if bought at a regular tobacconist's, cost a fortune.

He decided that the first cigarette of the day deserved to be a good one and, moving as little as possible, shook a Camel from its pack. There was a box of matches next to the cigarettes. He struck one, swore bitterly under his breath. What was there about France that she couldn't produce decent matches? Instead of wood for the match-sticks they used paper wrapped with wax. He struck another and made it this time.

Steve drew the first breath of life-giving smoke into his lungs, let it drift slowly through his nostrils. He looked from the side of his eyes at the girl. She had shifted slightly, was more nearly on her back. Her left breast was completely exposed now, its tip so red that Steve wondered whether or not she had put a cosmetic on it.

He couldn't care less. Just the sight of her next to him was all but nauseating. He wondered if it were always going to be this way. Put all your charm, all your energy and persuasiveness into convincing the girl that she was what you'd been looking for all your days. That nothing was more important than that they fulfill destiny by uniting in that most intimate relationship possible between two persons. Finally overwhelm all her defenses—not that most of them on the Riviera erected much in the way of defenses—and take her to bed.

And then kick her out in the morning.

Of course, it hadn't always been so. How long was it now? About five years. He wasn't a tourist representative then, living in a trailer parked upon an estate on the outskirts of Beaulieu, living a hedonistic bachelor's existence and probably undermining his health with too little exercise, too much drink, too much smoking and too many overly willing women. He was, face it, little more than an international bum now.

Then he'd been Mr. Steven Philip Cogswell, partner in the firm of Gunther & Cogswell, Efficiency Consultants.

* * * *

Steve Cogswell had known Martin Gunther for the greater part of their lives. The Gunther family had moved to El Monte, in southern California, when the boys were in the third and fifth grades respectively. A difference of two years is a considerable one at the age of eight and ten and Steve's first memories of Mart were those of an older kid who wasn't above imposing his will on his physical juniors.

However, by the time they were both attending the high school in Alhambra they'd managed to become buddies and there had been such shared experiences as the time they'd hitchhiked down to Tia Juana, in Mexico, without their parents' knowledge.

The two had considered themselves best friends by the time Mart Gunther went off to Columbia, back East, to study journalism. They'd corresponded off and on and then resumed the acquaintanceship when Steve took up studies for time-and-motion engineering at M.I.T.

It had been during a chance meeting, when both were working on assignments in Kingston, in upstate New York, that they'd hit upon the idea for their firm. Over beer in the Hofbrau Bar, they had given each other a rundown on their dissatisfaction with their present positions.

Steve was convinced that working for someone else was a mug's game if you had it on the ball to make a go of it by yourself. Mart was of the opinion that in a world that was becoming increasingly automated and efficient the newspaper field was falling behind and using methods more suited to the period preceding the First World War than that following the Second.

The idea must have hit them both at the same time. They stared at each other. Mart flicked a finger to the bartender for two more steins of beer, and they settled down to plan the firm of Gunther & Cogswell, Efficiency Consultants, specializing in the modernization of newspapers and publishing houses.

They'd had about five thousand dollars apiece to invest and it hadn't been enough, actually. Either that or the breaks hadn't come as quickly as they'd expected. In spite of the fact that they'd knocked themselves out trying to prove themselves, their jobs were far between.

What they needed was the one good chance. Just one fair-sized daily that would allow them to prove the value of installing the latest of printing equipment, redesigning the layout of pressroom floors, of bringing IBM machines into the accounting department—of all the hundred and one things they'd worked out in detail to cut both labor and equipment to a hone of efficiency.

The money melted away into office expenditures and into lengthy trips, usually undertaken by Steve, to interview this publisher, that editor, this manager of a newspaper chain. It melted away, and Steve watched it go and became increasingly tense, increasingly desperate, as he tried to prove himself.

He knew the idea was good; he was convinced of the validity of the basis of their firm. Already the journalistic field was feeling the pressure of radio and TV competition to the point where, unless changes were made, the newspaper would rapidly become a vestige of yesteryear.

There'd been just the three of them. Martin Gunther, Steven Cogswell and Mary Ballentine, the office girl. Four, counting Fay, who by this time was Steve's wife. Mart remained a bachelor.

Yes, you couldn't miss counting Fay. Fay Hanlon from Boston. Fay of the long legs, the striking body, the soft mouth, the arrogant breasts, the easy grace and practiced grooming, the air of the New England aristocrat, the Massachusetts accent so similar to the British. Yes, Fay the Boston aristocrat who had actually been born in the Chelsea section of town, the daughter of an Irish ward heeler. What Fay had, Fay had fought hard to get; every carefully pronounced word, every gesture of the gentlewoman, had been learned, not born into Fay.

But it took knowing her well, oh, so well, before you found that out.

You met Fay in the company of Boston's better people. You were charmed by her interests which so coincided with your own, by her keen perceptions, by her earnest beliefs in the things that counted.

You wondered how so attractive a girl could bother to be intellectually aware as well. Not, of course, that you ever forget her body, her heavy lips, her smoldering eyes—even while discussing politics and religion, art and ambition, and the true meaning of it all.

Steve remembered it so clearly.

He had taken his courage in hand and blurted, "Look, Miss Hanlon, I know I'm a bit out of line. We've only known each other a couple of hours but, well…"

Her eyes were wide; puzzled, but friendly. "Yes, Mr. Cogswell?"

Steve said, "Well, I'd like to see more of you."

She gestured vaguely, still puzzled, toward their host and hostess. "Why, I'm sure that through such mutual friends as the Morgans we'll cross paths from time to time."

"Well, look…I'm largely a stranger in town. I was—well, actually thinking of a date. Perhaps take in the Pop Opera some evening and then…"

Fay Hanlon seemed embarrassed by his impetuosity. "I don't know *what* to say, really. We're hardly acquainted, you know."

"Yes, but…" Steve had pursued eagerly.

And then, after the third date, he recalled how he had kissed her good night in front of the ultra-respectable woman's club in which she lived. Her lips had been soft, as they must be soft with such fullness, and her eyes, which smoldered so easily, had registered surprise, almost shock.

She had looked up at him for a moment, then down. She said, demurely, "But, Mr. Cogswell…Steven…"

He was taken aback by his own boldness. "I suppose I shouldn't have done that. I couldn't help myself, Fay."

She touched her lips with the tips of her fingers, then giggled, uncharacteristically. "You know, Steven, I don't believe I have been kissed since we played spin-the-bottle during a party in my grammar school days. My parents were furious when they found out." She turned quickly and sped into the building, calling a cheery good night.

Steve had stood looking after her, long after the door had closed.

Then, several months later, an evening had exploded into sex. There had been a rented convertible and Fay had gone much further than ever before. This was not the stolen kiss, this was not a brief moment of gentle, awkward caresses. This was Fay, a woman with a woman's needs, her dress hiked up to her hips, her voice moaning as he stroked her soft flesh.

Getting to the motel on the outskirts of Lynn and registering there, was all a blur. The only thing that registered on his mind was Fay.

He had never undressed a girl before. Nor undressed before one. His experience with sex had been minimal. Steve Cogswell had kept himself busy with schooling and then work. But she helped him, her eyes closed tightly and her voice incoherent.

"Steven, darling Steven. Please don't hurt me. You won't hurt me, will you, Steven?"

He had hoarsely tried to reassure her, even as his passion grew and he knew he was beyond the point where he could spare her. Then she was nude, all nude, and he, too, and for a moment he looked down on Fay. The breasts, the gently rounded belly, the cunning navel, the swell and glory of curved hips, the soft inner thighs, the long perfect legs.

Her eyes were closed, but she whispered, "I love you, Steven. It's only because I love you."

"I know," he said as gently as he could make it, and lowered himself upon her as her arms went around him hugging him close to her aching nakedness.

He was awakened in the morning by the sounds of her blubbering.

Fay crying? Fay the self-possessed? Fay the collected? Fay the perfect lady?

"Darling, what's the matter?" he had asked, bewildered.

Her eyes were tightly closed, her hands over her face, and it was difficult to make out the words that came through. "You'll never want to marry me now that I'm ruined...now that I'm not a virgin any more. You'll never respect me. Nobody will ever respect me.... I only allowed you, because I loved you.... I..."

Yes, Steve remembered it so clearly.

You looked at her in surprise, since you had never expected to see the self-possessed Fay in tears, not to speak of that cultured voice incoherent with shame and weeping. You told her about your love and respect, indeed your worship of her, and how the sooner you were married the better.

So you were wed. Steven Philip Cogswell, up-and-coming young efficiency engineer, with a good job with a good firm, a conscientious man well worth watching; and Fay Hanlon, of the Boston Hanlons, you know, an obvious aristocrat of the old school, undoubtedly of one of the very best families.

Fay hadn't much liked the idea of Gunther & Cogswell. She had fitted into the suburban life she and Steve had lived while he was still with the engineering company and with a steady and adequate income. The salary hadn't stretched quite so well as Steve had expected it to and Fay was continually suggesting he ask for raises. Still, she had been reasonably satisfied and Steve, of course, was head over heels in love with her.

A few illusions had dropped away with time. Fay wasn't quite the intellectual he had thought, nor were her interests so much in common with his own as he had believed. But she was still Fay and far and away the most attractive woman in the set in which they moved. Besides, she was all a man could handle in bed; all and a bit more when you were worn out from a frustrating day bumping your head up against a brick wall consisting of old-fashioned editors, outworn union featherbedding regulations, and stubborn publishers.

Gradually there had built up too many of those scenes where she'd find him, papers strewn over the desk in his study, immersed in his latest projected layout for a potential customer.

"You're not even dressed yet?" she'd say tightly.

"Dressed?" He'd look up at her vacantly. "Gosh, you look beautiful, honeybun."

Her foot would begin to tap. "The Hansens are throwing a party tonight. You promised…"

"Good grief, I forgot." His eyes would go desperate. "Look, Fay. I've simply got to have this ready tomorrow. As it is, I'll be up until two or three o'clock. Why don't you just go and make my apologies?"

Or, even worse, the times when he'd come stumbling home, eyes glazed with fatigue, to find Fay waiting for him, already in negligee. Fay had a way of letting something that had happened during the day stimulate her—some TV show she'd watched, perhaps a movie with a favorite sex-symbol male star. At times like this her needs were all-demanding, and increasingly often at times like this, it was impossible for Steve to give her fulfillment.

Then it had all fallen apart one day. All at once.

In memory, it was very clear.

Steve Cogswell had returned in the late afternoon from an unhappy interview with Mike Farnsworth, editor-in-chief of the Hammett chain of weeklies which spread over New England. The Hammett chain consisted of a score of small-town papers, but they sold ad space to the national advertisers as a bloc and thus were able to guarantee a total circulation of several hundred thousand.

Steve had tried to convince Farnsworth that the chain ought to carry this co-operation one step further. That the whole chain ought to be printed in one centrally located, ultra-modern shop, thus saving duplication of body type and ad setting, and all using the same cartoon strips, advice-to-the-lovelorn columns and such. Only the front page, the editorial page and local news would differ in each paper. It was a complicated scheme. Steve had worked it out in detail—but Mike Farnsworth hadn't bought it.

Steve said to the office girl, "Back a day sooner than I'd expected, Mary. How's it going?"

Mary Ballentine said, her voice strange, "Nothing new, Mr. Cogswell."

"Where's Mr. Gunther?"

"I dont know, sir."

He frowned at her. "Do you have a cold or something, Mary?"

"No, sir."

Steve said, "Fay's not here either, huh? Wasn't there work enough to keep her busy?"

"I suppose not." Mary Ballentine refrained from looking at the large pile of mailing she had on her desk and at which she'd been busily working.

In a way, right then, Steve knew. His mind went blank, unthinking. He left the office without speaking further to Mary Ballentine, got into his car and drove home. He parked a half-block away and walked the remaining distance. He entered by the back door. It was a small house, but in a good neighborhood and ultramodern throughout. They had been in it only six months. *Nineteen years of payments still to go*, Steve thought dully.

They hadn't even had the decency to perform their sexual gyrations in some neutral zone. They were on the bed, in the bed, all over the bed—in Steve and Fay's room.

Mart Gunther looked up, his face chalky, his eyes wide and stricken. "My God, Stevie," he blurted, "I can explain this!"

That was too much. Too utterly, flatly, incongruously too much. Steve Cogswell began to laugh. A broken and all but hysterical laugh.

Save for one stocking and her garter belt, Fay was nude. Beautifully, wonderfully nude, as only Fay could be. The body, the one and only body, that Steve Cogswell had come to love so desperately.

Save for his small, tight, European-type briefs, Mart Gunther was nude too. Steve wondered, even as he laughed, what the other offered Fay that he, Steve, couldn't.

The man was no Olympic star, physically. In fact, his waist was already getting on the heavy side, and his body, untouched by the sun this summer, was a lardy white.

It was obvious that the man had already been aroused by the time Steve Cogswell had entered the room. With the removal of the remaining stocking and the garter belt—a matter of moments probably, since the bed had a disheveled, clothes-strewn appearance that denoted passion and haste—their act of love would have been speedily consummated.

Act of love? Steve's laughter choked off.

Raw, meaningless, animal sex. Two animal bodies grinding together, reaching the crest of emotional climax together. A sow in heat and a rutting boar to serve her. It had no more meaning than that.

Mart Gunther rolled away in such wise as to be at the far side of the bed from Steve. His face was pasty and his lips drawn back so that his teeth showed.

Had Steve likened him to a boar? A fearful rat was the better term. He was not even thinking in terms of protecting the woman with whom he'd been in lust the moment before.

"Now listen, Stevie," he said again, his voice high. "Don't do anything until you give me—us—a chance to explain."

What did he expect, for Steve to begin shooting?

And that was when Fay had exploded.

Fay the aristocrat. Fay of the controlled voice. Fay of the Boston Hanlons. Fay the groomed. Fay the lady. To Steve's confused mind came the meaningless phrase, *Fay the Lily-Maid of Astolat.*

Fay exploded and from her white lips, from that horrible gash in her hate-filled face, from that twisting, hating tongue came a stream of obscenity that sent Steve Cogswell back a full step in shock.

And then some of her sentences, her incoherent phrases, began to make sense.

"You cheap, undersexed jerk... You half-man... What have you got to complain about? ... You can't do it. .... You can't make a woman feel it, like it. .... What the hell do you care if somebody else does the job for you? ... Why, I've had kids in high school knew how to jazz better than you....

"All this crap about the beauty of my soul and this fiddling around, and petting, and admiring my goddess-like body like you

call it. ... *My goddess-like body, hell ... I'm a woman. A woman, understand? ... Do you know what a woman is, you sad sack? ... Get out of here! ... Get out of here and let a man, a man with something on his mind besides work, work, work, do what a man's supposed to do. ...*

"*To hell with your work ... To hell with you sitting around in the evenings with your plans and your layouts and your— How I hate a man who can't perform in the saddle! ... How I've hated to be married to a cheap creep who doesn't know how to handle a woman. ... God, how I've loved cheating on you, Steven Philip Cogswell!*"

There had been more. It was still going on when he stumbled from the room.

He hadn't known. He hadn't had the slightest idea...

* * * *

Steve Cogswell finished his cigarette, staring up at the trailer's ceiling as he smoked. Now the girl beside him was stirring. Confound it, he couldn't remember her name. The tourists came down at the rate of sixty-seven a week, in season, and it was just beyond him to remember them all.

Of course, he'd been at the party with her the night before, but he couldn't remember the night before. Not beyond the point when that fluttery Dave Shepherd had rung in the bottle of absinthe. Steve could only remember drinking the first frappé—and he'd probably had more.

The girl's eyes opened and she smiled sleepily at him. "Morning, Steven," she purred.

Purred was the correct word. She was a kitten. Blond as blond, wide and blue of eye. Rounded and silken white—in spite of the two weeks on the Riviera. Steve decided wryly that she'd probably spent more time in bed than on the beach.

Steve ground out the cigarette butt in the tray next to the bed and attempted to keep his voice pleasant. "We'll have to get going," he said "I've got to get all you holiday-makers together and down to Nice in time for the plane to London."

The blonde pouted at him. "Don't I even get a morning kiss, lover?" She half-closed her eyes, slumberously, but at the same time made a girlish attempt to cover her revealed breasts.

Steve rolled from the bed, relieved to find he was wearing the bottom half of pajamas. "You're a glutton," he told her, hoping his voice was light and that she wouldn't take offense. "Look, I'll slip into the bathroom first and get organized. I'm simply fanny-deep in work on a Friday morning. I've got to run into Monaco."

"Not even time for a spot of breakfast?" she wailed.

He had pulled out a drawer and was fishing forth fresh clothing. Faded blue linen slacks, a Madras sport shirt—official attire on the Côte d'Azur. He brought out rope-soled sandals, colorful socks.

She was saying, looking about the small trailer room, "Goodness, you Yankees really take your caravans seriously. How large is this, anyway?"

"Twenty-eight feet," Steve muttered. "It's not considered particularly big in the States."

"But a bathroom, and a fridge in the kitchen, and TV and armchairs there in the living room, and that little bar. Why, it's just like a real home."

"It's the only home I've got," Steve said drily. Damn, but he wished she'd shut up.

"And all aluminum," she wondered. "Did you bring it from the States with you?"

He shook his head, his hand on the bathroom door. He had to be polite to this blister. It was bad policy for him to mess around with the Far Away Holidays clients. Antagonize one and they could put in a beef to the head office in London. Too many complaints and that'd be the end of this job, and if there was anything Steve Cogswell didn't want it was to have to leave the Riviera, looking for some other employment.

Decent jobs weren't a dime a dozen for an American in Europe, and particularly in France. You needed a work permit to take a job in France and to get it you had to prove it was a position a Frenchman couldn't hold down.

In this case, John Brett-James, the boss up in England, had claimed his customers felt more secure if their Riviera representative was either British or American, and France, of course, bent over backward to baby the tourist trade.

Steve said, "I bought it from a couple of rich tourists who brought it over and then didn't want to be bothered with the rigmarole of shipping it back." He could have added, but didn't, *"Your friend Conny Kamiros lent me the money."*

He went into the bathroom, hurried through a shave and shower, dressed and then emerged.

She was still in bed. He said, "I'm going to have to scoot. Your hotel is the Ruhl, in Nice, isn't it? When you're dressed, you can go up to the villa and the contessa will call a cab for you. You'd better hurry. The plane arrives at eleven and you'll have to be at the airport at least an hour ahead of time."

She was half-scowling at him, and began to say something, but he ignored it and left the trailer and headed toward the villa himself.

It was a beautiful day, as all days are beautiful on the Côte d'Azur in August. Behind him, the blue-green Mediterranean, unbelievably clear, sparkled in the morning sun. To his left was Cap Ferrat, with Saint Jean snuggling on the peninsula. To his right was the semitropical town of Beaulieu; Little Africa the old-timers called it, the warmest town come winter on the Riviera.

The Contessa Carla Rossi had her estate charmingly situated between the two small resorts and with a small private beach, one of the best in the vicinity. It was a break for Steve, being able to park his trailer down near the beach and slightly to one side, his electric and water outlets hitched up to the unused gardener's cottage. A break for which he was properly thankful. The regular tourist parking grounds at this time of year were a crowded horror and the beaches near them unusable.

He climbed the score or more stone steps that wound up the rocky way to the main house and strolled across the lawn to the French windows of what had once been one of the proudest villas on the Riviera and was now the Pavilion Budapest, an ultra-swank pension operated by Carla Rossi. The contessa, like so many of the Riviera's titled folk had fallen on harsh times.

Not so harsh as all that, however. Her former Italian banker husband, now deceased, had been an ardent admirer of Matisse and of Picasso, before those artists had drawn the world's acclaim. Most of his friends had thought Conte Rossi was doing the painters a philanthropy when he bought their works at a few thousand frances a throw. There were at least a dozen prime examples of the work of each in the Pavilion Budapest, and had the contessa sold one or two of them, she would certainly have had no need to rent out her home to tourist guests. But that wasn't the contessa's style. Hardly.

Carla Rossi was in the swank, crystal-chandeliered living room when Steven entered. She was dressed in black Capri pants, a soft blue pullover, and with matching blue velvet ballet shoes. The contessa was probably in the vicinity of forty but her figure was that of a nineteen-year-old—and she knew it.

She was standing, hands on hips, legs spread, and glaring ruefully at the wreckage of last night's party. She looked at him when he entered, her face impish. The contessa reminded Steve of the Gabor sisters—Zsa Zsa, probably. Which wasn't too far out since Carla Rossi had been bora in Hungary. She said to him, "Carla is beginning to think that the tourist business isn't worth it."

"Ha," he said.

"What is this ha, you wolf?"

"You wouldn't know what to do with yourself, unless you ran this place. Besides, you love to throw parties and can't afford it. So you need these suckers to pony up the money." Steve scowled at her. "What do you mean, wolf?"

"I saw you with poor Conny's girl last night. That awful blond witch."

Steve made a face. "She'll be up here in a few minutes. Get her a cab and get rid of her, won't you, Carla?"

"Ha," she snorted. "The same as ever, eh? Last night she was the darling. This morning she disgusts you." She looked at him archly. "Carla is glad we have never got around to a—what do you Americans call it?—a roll in the hay. I am afraid our friendship would not survive it, Steve."

She was speaking the truth, as a matter of fact, and Steve knew it, but he only grunted, "See you later, honey bun."

He made his way toward the side door which led toward the villa's garages. At the door he met Dave Shepherd, snorkle and flippers in hand and dressed in a flaming pair of bathing trunks. Dave was a semipermanent resident at the Pavilion Budapest.

Steve pretended to wince at the bright color. "That outfit will scare away all the fish," he protested. "Skin diving is bad enough in this area already."

Dave giggled. "My dear," he said. "Do you *really* like them?"

"No," Steve said flatly. "See you later, everybody."

Dave called after him, "Oh, you have no *taste*, dear boy."

Steve grunted something to that under his breath and made his way to the garage. His Citroën ID station wagon was neck to neck with the contessa's aged Rolls and half a dozen cars ranging from a Thunderbird to a Lancia belonging to current residents.

* * * *

He took the shoreline Corniche into Monaco, about ten kilometers, or six miles, to the east, passing through the harbor-side resort of Beaulieu and later through Eze-s Mer on the way.

Where France ended and Monaco began was hard to tell. The tiny principality, some 370 acres in all, half the size of New York's Central Park, had neither border guards nor customs. You were in France one moment, and Monaco the next, and who was to care?

He drove down Boulevard Princess Charlotte to Avenue du Berceau and turned left, parked the Citroën as near to the tiny office of Far Away Holidays as he could and traversed the rest of the way on foot.

Elaine Marimbert had already opened up this morning, as she usually did. She was a cute little Monegasque, one of the less than three thousand citizens of the tiny nation, and as proud of her country as though it had been a world power.

Monegasque she might be by nationality but French she was in language, in cultural background, and in the undeniably Gallic appearance she boasted. These days, in common with some twenty million Frenchwomen, she was copying the hair-do, the pertness, and the flashing eyes of Brigitte Bardot and on her it couldn't have looked better. Petite, chic, ultra-modern, she was a decided asset to Far Away Holidays and Steve appreciated her, even though her hobby did seem to be snidely heckling him.

It was because of her value as an assistant that he had never allowed the girl's charms to impress themselves upon him. He had seen her eye his six-foot, lanky form, run her eyes over his open, typically American face, and there had been approval in her glance.

But Steve knew what would result. They'd wind up in bed, sooner or later, and that would be the end of their relationship and probably result in her quitting her job. He just couldn't be more than coolly polite to a woman once she'd surrendered to him.

Today Elaine wore the sport clothes the weather demanded, a cleverly designed dress in the latest style down from Paris, and clever sandals, probably from across the nearby border in Italy.

Elaine looked up at him as he entered. *"Bon jour, Monsieur Cogswell."*

"Speak English," Steve told her, but smiling his own greeting. "You need the practice. Any crises this morning?"

"Mr. Kamiros called. He wants you to call back. There's a cable from London. Two of the tourists scheduled to stay at the Venise et Continental, in Menton, canceled at the last minute. There'll be only sixty-five on the plane today."

"Damn it," Steve growled, "that's the third last-minute cancellation for that hotel in the past month. Jules will be a hornet."

Elaine said mildly, "At this time of the year he shouldn't have any trouble filling his rooms with casuals off the street."

Steve said, "A hotel manager likes to know where he stands, not to depend on last-minute guests dropping in. What did Conny want?"

"He didn't say, Monsieur Cogswell. Should I get him?"

"I suppose so," Steve said. He had a premonition that he wasn't going to like what Conny Kamiros was going to say.

He didn't. The Greek gambler's voice was as soft as usual, but what he said hurt. He wanted, in brief, the five thousand dollars Steve owed him.

Steve sputtered, "Hell, Conny, you know I don't have that kind of money on hand. I was figuring on paying you back a thousand at a time over a period of several years."

"That was before my rather inflated ego was sandpapered, my friend," the Greek tycoon said softly.

Steve said in irritation, "Well, I haven't got it, Conny, and you can't get blood out of this particular turnip. I'll pay you as soon as I can."

"I'm afraid that's not soon enough, Steve."

"It'll have to be."

Constantine Kamiros said evenly, "When I sent you over to Nick to pick up the loan you wanted, what kind of paper did you sign, Steve?"

Oh, oh! Steve Cogswell sent his mind back. It was one thing, the easygoing Conny shrugging his heavy shoulders and telling Steve he'd be happy to let him have five thousand with which to buy the American trailer that was available for a song. But it was another thing when you confronted his secretary-business manager, Nicholas Lindos, not exactly famous as being a quick man with a buck—no matter what currency was involved.

Nick had drawn up papers using the trailer, Steve's Citroën, and for all practical purposes the clothes on his back, as collateral. And Nick had been bitter, even then. He hadn't thought that Steve's all was enough backing for a loan of that magnitude. Not that Steve had worried. Conny had told his friend that he was in no hurry and even hinted that if Steve never paid him back, he wouldn't mind.

He thought Steve would like the trailer and he wanted him to have it. It fitted in with Steve's way of life. Work on the Riviera with the tourists for six or seven months of the year and then batting around Europe for the remainder, living it up, drinking it up, wenching on the grand scale.

Steve said now, "Look, Conny, I've got to get my tourists together and get them off to London, then I've got to meet the incoming plane with the new batch. Can we talk this over later?"

"Any time at all, Steve," the Greek said smoothly. "Sorry to bother you about such mundane things." He hung up.

"Oh, Lord," Steve grumbled. He turned to Elaine, who had been pretending not to listen, but who now had a distressed expression on her face. "Elaine, take over. Phone all the hotels where we have tourists and be sure arrangements have been made to get them to the airport. Be particularly sure that pair of lesbians at the Mira-monte are rounded up. They're as nutty as fruitcakes and probably don't realize it's Friday. I'll pick up the clients we have at the Pavilion Budapest in my station wagon. Right?"

"Okay," Elaine said. With her Provençal accent, it came out, "Okéy."

Steve hurried out to the Citroën and tooled it back in the direction of Beaulieu. That damn Conny! He was probably as mad as a Russian diplomat at the United Nations. Steve would have to figure out some way to smooth things over. He knew the Greek basically liked him, and he returned the feeling.

At the Nice-Côte d'Azur airport, Steve Cogswell had his average handful of confusion. Sixty-seven of the Far Away Holidays vacationists had to be shepherded together, their luggage and gift purchases all organized and then given a final farewell talk and hustled into the departing passengers' waiting room. Once in there, he was safe. There was no way they could escape. His responsibilities were over. Next stop, London, and the boys there could take over.

Sixty-five new tourists were incoming on the turbo-jet Viscount which Far Away Holidays chartered each week for the London-Riviera run, to take one batch of clients, pick up another. The Viscount was one of the neatest tricks in air travel. Four turbo-props, three stewardesses, two large rest rooms, and excellent cuisine; the British United Airlines, which leased the craft to the tourist concern, did themselves proud.

Most of Steve's clients were fairly experienced travelers who utilized the package vacations because of both economy and the efficiency with which its representatives took over the everyday worries of foreign travel.

No need to bother with customs, passports, hotel reservations, tipping, selecting restaurants and all the rest of the routine. Far Away Holidays handled it all. The swankest in international living-it-up for a mere seventy pounds a week—less than two hundred dollars—including transportation to and from London. You couldn't beat it.

The experienced ones gave Steve little trouble. They knew the ropes and were inclined to take things in stride. The emergencies came with the first-trippers—those who had never been out of England or the United States, as the case might be, and were flustered at being in a foreign country.

When they disembarked, Steve led them to a medium-sized waiting room, picking up their passports from one of the stewardesses who had gathered them up in flight. He submitted the passports—the American ones green, the British, blue—for French inspection and gave orders for the luggage to be brought into customs. Then he stood up on a handy bench and gave them a short talk.

It was routine. Explanation of the local money and what the new French franc was worth in terms of dollars and pounds. Explanation of the fact that the new franc was worth one hundred times as much as the old one. Explanation of how Far Away Holidays buses would take them to their respective hotels in Nice, Monaco or Menton. He distributed a small brochure which listed side tours they could take. He gave them a brief rundown on the value of his tours of the night clubs and casinos, warned the single ladies about gigolos and pick-ups on the beaches, warned the single men about ladies of the evening—all with an amused smirk, of course, which brought the expected giggles and snickers.

By the time the luggage was through customs and the passports stamped, Steve Cogswell had come to the end of his little speech. He wound up by taking the passenger list and reading off their names, telling each, in turn, in which hotel he was scheduled to stay.

The last name of the list was Nadine Whiteley, who was to stay at the Pavilion Budapest. It was the first time Steve Cogswell became aware of the existence of Nadine Whiteley, but it was a name destined to loom largely in his immediate future.

CHAPTER TWO

Saturday, August 6th

Nadine Whiteley drifted into that half-land between sleep and waking. It was early morning, she was aware, and already the heat of the coming day was warmly comfortable.

She didn't want to awaken and enter the world of reality. She was conscious of the fact that the bed in which she lay was a strange one. Where was she? She didn't want to emerge completely from sleep, but she did wonder where she was. And when. What had happened yesterday?

She entered a sort of game which she had played with herself since early childhood when she emerged from sleep into this half-dream state. She started at the first memory that came immediately to her and worked forward in time from that point.

Even in her semi-sleep a pang struck her. Her father's death. Now she was alone. Her mother had died twenty-seven years ago when Nadine had been born. And now Dad was gone and Nadine was sole owner of the furniture factory, and, for all practical purposes, of the little semi-feudalistic town which housed it. For three generations the Whiteleys had owned Samara—the factory, the land, the houses, even the stores. It was a type of factory town rapidly disappearing in the United States, but still to be found occasionally in New England and more often in the South.

But she could remember more recently than that. Ah, yes. The party at the artist's house in Woodstock and meeting Gerald Silletoe. She stirred uncomfortably in her half-sleep. Jerry Silletoe—big, squarely handsome, unusually well groomed and with a sophistication far beyond that of Nadine, who, except for school, had seen little beyond the Catskills.

She had never really found out anything about Silletoe, but his background struck her as vaguely sinister from the beginning—an impression increased by the fact that he never talked about it.

He once let slip the fact that his childhood had been spent on the tougher streets of Brooklyn, but later denied even this. He never referred to his occupation or source of income, and she never met any of his friends. That day in Woodstock she heard hints from other guests that Silletoe had underworld connections, but she dismissed the rumors because one just didn't meet gangsters at artists' cocktail parties.

Still there *was* something brutal about the way he carried his big body and a glint of cruelty lurked in his dark, probing eyes. Once during the party, when the conversation veered to a certain notorious mobster who was currently having income tax trouble, she caught an expression of cynical amusement and cunning flicker across Silletoe's heavy face. It occurred to Nadine for a crazy instant that if there was any role this man seemed custom-built for, it was that of a crime syndicate hood—smooth, secretive and ruthless.

Yet she had found him fascinating, and dismissed her misgivings as girlish fantasy. She was probably just romanticizing the man's aura of potent sensuality, the sense of violence which actually excited her.

However, his behavior at their final scene together tended to confirm her dark suspicions. There was definitely something lawless and dangerous about Jerry Silletoe.

She stirred now, uncomfortably, as that scene came back to her. She hadn't discouraged him. How could she have been expected to? She was twenty-seven years of age. Twenty-seven and fully normal, with a woman's body and a woman's instincts and capacity for love, lacking only in experience.

It had taken place in the living room of the big house in Samara after Martha and William had gone to bed. In the big house atop the hill and overlooking the town. For a time caught up in the excitement and the passion, caught up in the engulfing needs of her body and in the compelling forcefulness of Jerry's demanding arms and lips and his caressing hands. For a time wanting him, needing him, waiting for him.

Then the stark terror at the actual moment of reception. The startled surprise in Jerry's face. Then, as the fear swept her and rose higher and higher and she beat at his naked chest with her clenched fists, beat at him and cried her refusal. How then his expression of surprise had turned to impatience and then dull anger, and he had tried to force her.

She screamed in hysteria, terrified at the threat of penetration. "No! Please, God, no!"

"Stop it!" he growled. His voice was savage. "It's too late, now!" He held her down.

"No!" Her voice broke and the words became incoherent, but her screams climbed in a crescendo of fright.

William and Martha, incongruously dressed in the night-clothes of half a century ago, were at the door and suddenly the room was bright with light.

"Sir!" William had shouted, his aged voice high with alarm and anger. He hurried forward, his feet shuffling in ancient slippers. "Miss Nadine…are you all right?"

Jerry Silletoe had come to his feet, his clothes still disarranged, his face dark with anger. "Get out of here," he said heavily, dangerously, to William.

"Sir," the old man said tremulously but defiantly, "I must order you to leave immediately or I shall summon the authorities."

Martha was comforting Nadine, trying to rearrange her clothing. It must have looked like sheer rape to the elderly servants. Her brassiere was stripped from her body, her skirts up about bare white thighs.

Jerry's eyes had gone from Nadine to the servants, and savagely back. He muttered some obscenity and strode rapidly toward the door.

Now, Nadine squirmed in her semi-sleep, wanting even less to emerge into full wakefulness. The horror of it, the disgrace of it. William and Martha had been aghast.

And the following day Nadine had gone to old Dr. Levine, who had brought her into the world and her mother before her.

She had told him her story from the beginning. From the very beginning. Of Uncle Nathaniel and the time he was more than ordinarily drunk and Nadine no more than twelve years of age. Her mind tried to refuse the memory, but she knew it had happened in all its disgusting detail.

She'd been alone in the house with Uncle Nat, and, as usual by this time of evening, he had been well into a quart of the locally produced applejack. She had come into the living room wearing nothing but her bathrobe, the summer heat being such that everyone slept nude. She should have seen sooner that something was wrong.

She had sat on his lap, artlessly, and didn't particularly mind when he had, seemingly unconsciously, stroked her legs and caressed her even then rounded bottom, as he talked to her.

Then he had pretended to make it a game.

"Do you ever let the boys touch you there?"

"Uncle Nat! Don't do that."

"Or kiss you like this?"

At first there had been a timid curiosity, and then she had let him go beyond the turning point. She could still remember scraps of the conversation—if it could be called conversation.

"Oh, no, Uncle Nat. Oh, please don't. I'll tell father. Don't hurt me. No…oh, no. It's so big. No, no, please…"

Afterward, there was the pain and the fright, and the blood on her legs and clothing. Still later, Uncle Nat, had gone stumbling off to drive his car full tilt into the Ashokan Reservoir. On purpose? She'd never know. Before that night of horror, he'd been her favorite relative.

Dr. Levine had listened to the full recital. Of how she had progressed through the usual high school and college romances, but never going further than light petting. Of her underlying fear of ever going further than perhaps a secretly fondled breast. Then Roger Stuart and their engagement, which had lasted a full six months and had terminated only days before the wedding when they had decided to consummate it with a premarital experiment.

It was then, on the lawn of the Stuart family, that Nadine had discovered that sex was not for her. Until the moment of attempted penetration, she was seemingly normal, as desirous of fulfillment as the most passionate. But then it became so utterly impossible, and the hysteria struck. Instead of gentle, easygoing, goodlooking Roger, her fiancé, it suddenly seemed to become Uncle Nat, and the pain, and the fear, and the blood, and then, next morning, the news of his accident—or suicide.

Dr. Levine had listened to it. Old, tired Dr. Levine, who had seen all of life in his nearly seventy years—had seen it all and been saddened by it.

He had told her gently that she was a beautiful, sensitive woman, needful of love and needful of satisfying the normal sexual appetites of her body. He recommended she see a psychiatrist in New York. Before that, however, he pointed out to her that although he could hardly recommend she have an affair out of wedlock, it would not be fair for her ever to marry under existing conditions. Her husband-to-be couldn't become aware of her neurosis, of her fear of the act of love, except on the night of their wedding. This must be conquered before marriage....

Nadine was beginning to emerge from her half-sleep now, beginning to remember where she was. She hadn't taken the doctor's advice about the psychiatrist. She couldn't face revealing her experiences to an outsider.

Instead, she had coolly planned a campaign to settle her difficulties. She must leave Samara for it. She could hardly risk the possibility of more scandal. It had been bad enough that William and Martha had seen her with Jerry.

So she had conceived the trip to the French Riviera. She was to be here a week. During that time she would find a stranger, an attractive man without strings. One who would welcome a short holiday affair with an American girl. One who knew nothing of her background, would make no demands upon her and expect her to make none on him.

Now she was suddenly wide-awake.

She was here at last. The jet flight across the Atlantic was behind her, and the two days in London where she had picked up her Far Away Holidays reservation for the package luxury vacation. The trip down on the Viscount. Their being met at the airport by that pleasant-looking tourist representative who had given them the amusing little talk about enjoying themselves on the Riviera. And then the drive here to her room at the Pavilion Budapest. It had been a beautiful drive from Nice, the Mediterranean, impossibly clear, on the one side, the mountains of Provence on the other.

Nadine Whiteley looked up at the ceiling high above her. This villa, the Pavilion Budapest, she decided must have once been a very wealthy person's joy. It had the antique beauty of yesteryear, the furnishings and paintings, the drapes and rugs of an era more ostentatious perhaps than our own, but with a comfortable beauty that our present generation has lost.

For a brief moment, she allowed herself to doubt. The scheme was all so fantastic. Imagine flying three thousand miles with no purpose in mind other than deliberately allowing oneself to be seduced. Why, it was ridiculous!

No, it wasn't. She steeled herself. She was twenty-seven years of age and had all the normal instincts in regards to love and off-spring. She had every reason to believe that she would make a desirable wife, a devoted mother. She owed it to herself, to her eventual husband, and to the children to come. She *must*, some-how, break this barrier. She was convinced that if she could bring herself to the act, just once, only once, then forever after her fears of sex would be gone.

Nadine sat upright, swung her legs about and to the floor and came to her feet, stretching. She wore a short nightgown and for a wicked moment wondered how her sought-for lover would feel if he could see her now.

Had she known it, he would have been moved indeed. Nadine Whiteley, at twenty-seven, was the epitome of American woman-hood. Her breasts were high and full, her waist captivatingly nar-row, her hips blooming out, to flow, in turn, into legs that would have shamed any Venus ever laved by the waters of the Mediter-ranean.

She hustled to the bath and began her preparations for her cam-paign.

* * * *

Steve Cogswell reflected with satisfaction that Carla's little stretch of beach was one of the best this side of Cannes. Actually, contrary to popular belief, Riviera beaches are strictly second-rate compared to those of Florida, California or Hawaii. Nice, so fa-mous as a resort, has such a narrow one, and so pebbly, that it is all but impossible, in season, to find a spot to recline and all but unbearable on the feet to walk down to the water. The small Monte Carlo beach is man-made and has continually to have more sand dumped upon it.

But the contessa's property was one of the most favorably lo-cated for miles around. Guests swam in a cove, a half-acre of sand so shielded by rocky cliffs on both sides that prying eyes were forever barred. Not that nude bathing was practical, usually, since there were twenty or so paying guests at the Pavilion Budapest at any given time and the waters of the Mediterranean were attractive to them all.

As a matter of fact, one of them was approaching now. A bi-kini-clad girl whom Steve vaguely placed as one of his Far Away Holidays tourists who had arrived the day before. What was her name, now? He couldn't remember, in spite of the fact that he had driven her over from the airport himself. An American girl, as he recalled, but, confound it, what was her name? The tourists liked you to have their names on the tip of your tongue.

He emerged from the water and took up his towel as she approached.

"Morning," he called. "Beautiful day for a swim."

She smiled back. "Are you leaving? I'm not driving you away, am I? Let me see, you're Mr. Cogswell."

"Steve Cogswell," he said, taking in her figure, and telling himself that here was a girl who was really *stacked*. Whoever had invented the bikini had surely had this sort of thing in mind. Her figure was that of Elizabeth Taylor, her face that of Ingrid Bergman back when that star had been in her twenties. He toweled himself quickly. "I have to get into the office in Monte Carlo, Miss…"

"Nadine Whiteley," she replied. Less obviously than he, she had taken in his own masculine figure. In spite of the hedonistic life of the past few years, Steve Cogswell in his early thirties still cut a pleasing figure in his Hawaiian-style bathing shorts. He made a point of daily swims, occasional tennis at the Sports Club in Monaco, and fifteen minutes each morning with weights. It countered his admittedly too heavy drinking.

He stopped for a moment to converse with her. Already he could feel stirring within him the prerogatives of manhood. Confound it, he was going to have to watch himself with clients. He couldn't afford to do his compulsive catting around with Far Away Holidays customers. In the long run that would prove to be job suicide.

He said, "How do you find the Pavilion Budapest?"

"Wonderful," she told him, sinking to the sand and looking up. "I met the contessa at breakfast. Is she really a countess?"

"That she is," Steve said. "In fact, she carries some sort of Hungarian title, too. She became a refugee when the Soviets overran Hungary in 1944 and met the count, Giuseppe Rossi, in Switzerland. From what they say, the count was quite an old boy but he's been dead now for seven or eight years."

"She seems very clever."

"That she is," Steve said again. "Look, Miss Whiteley, I'll have to get along. Were you interested in taking any of the special tours? I have to make up my lists."

"I think I'd like to make that trip down to Nîmes for the bull-fight, but none of the others. When it comes to night-clubbing and sight-seeing, I'd rather be on my own." For what she had in mind, Nadine had decided, that sounded like much the better plan.

The Nîmes trip it is," Steve said. "Anything else I can do to make your holiday a success?"

She frowned thoughtfully, the slight wrinkles giving her a charming expression which Steve knew couldn't be artful. She had a piquant face, expressive and openly honest. He couldn't take his eyes from the manner in which her lips tucked in at the corners.

"How difficult is it to rent a car?" she queried.

"Not at all. A little expensive though."

"Oh, that's not important."

"Well, there's a place in Monaco—the Sporting Garage on Boulevard de France where you might rent a Simca. I'll take you in if you want."

"Wonderful, but I haven't had my dip yet and you're all ready to go."

"I haven't had breakfast," Steve said. "If you're ready by the time I am, it's a deal. Otherwise I'm afraid I'll have to push along. This is my busiest morning."

She dashed for the water, saying over her shoulder, "Expect me!"

By the time Steve was ready to go, Nadine was sitting in the front seat of the Citroën, much to his approval. He wasn't particularly fond of tourists who made him toady to their lack of punctuality, not when you considered that he had almost seventy of them on hand at any given time.

Their conversation was animated on the short trip into Monte Carlo. When she mentioned that she came from the Catskills, he told her of the job he'd once held in Kingston. It turned out that they had mutual friends in the nearby art colony of Woodstock.

She was somewhat taken aback by the fact that he had once held down a job as an efficiency engineer with a major firm but was now simply a tourist representative on the Riviera.

He grinned at her ruefully. "Miss Whiteley—"

"Nadine."

"Nadine," he said, "you must never ask an expatriate why he has become a modernized version of a beachcomber on the Côte d'Azur. It's something like the Foreign Legion. It's bad manners to ask about a person's past."

They laughed together and swept into Monaco at a pleasant clip. Traffic this early in the morning was light and speed possible. Steve gave her a brief rundown on the sights in the tiny country. He pointed out The Rock, upon which was Monaco-Ville, the oldest part of the town, and the palace of the former Grace Kelly and her prince.

Beyond lay La Condamine, which faced the port so filled with yachts from all over the world. Riding at anchor was Aristotle Onassis' converted destroyer escort, one of the most elaborate pleasure ships afloat. Beyond the yacht basin was Monte Carlo, most famed of all Riviera resort towns.

The Boulevard de France, Nadine's destination, was but a few blocks beyond the Far Away Holidays office and Steve drove her down to the Place de La Cremaillère, onto the boulevard and to the office of the Sporting Garage.

"They speak English here," he said. "Ask for Pierre Jacquin. He'll take care of you. See you later, Nadine."

She waved her thanks and good-by and he was off.

At the office, Elaine Marimbert was looking a bit on the harried side as she murmured, "yes, yes, indeed, sir, oh, yes, I'll take care of it immediately," into the phone. When she saw Steve she cast her eyes upward in mock despair but continued her soothing efforts into the mouthpiece.

When she'd hung up, Steve said, while going rapidly through the mail on his desk. "What's the crisis?"

"One of the tourists at the Hôtel de Paris complaining about his room."

Steve grunted his disgust. "It's the best hotel in Monaco."

"He says he was promised a different view when he made his reservations in London."

"Well, give René a ring and see what he can do. I know the type. Next he'll complain about the food and probably the wine. There's at least one in every planeload."

Elaine said cautiously, "Mr. Lindos called and left a message."

"Nick Lindos, Conny's secretary? What did he want?"

Elaine cleared her throat unhappily. "He said Mr. Kamiros had given you one week. Then he'll have to foreclose."

Steve winced.

He looked at his watch. There was nothing he could do about

Conny now. He had to see his clients. If you didn't catch them at mealtime, at their hotels, you didn't catch them period. They scattered around to the beaches, to the cafés, to the shops—and to each other's beds—to the point where it was absolutely impossible to round them up. And this was the day he sold them the special tours.

"Well, take over, Elaine," he told her. I'm off to Menton. I'll cover the hotel there as quickly as possible and perhaps return here in time for the Hôtel de Paris. I've already seen the clients at the Pavilion Budapest."

"How is it going so far?" Elaine said, picking up the ringing phone.

"Average. Looks like we'll have quite a few for the Nîmes bullfight. Probably have to rent a bus. Is that anything important?"

She put her hand over the mouthpiece. "Somebody with a British accent asking for you. He sounds indignant about something."

"Tell him I just left," Steve flung over his shoulder as he hustled out the door.

* * * *

Menton was no more than six kilometers—about three and a half miles—to the east. Flush on the Italian border, it was the last town on the French Riviera and one of the most attractive. Steve had fourteen of the Far Away Holidays tourists quartered here this planeload.

Twelve of them showed up for breakfast while he was there and he was able to check on their satisfaction with their accommodations and to get them lined up for the various side trips and night club tours which he offered.

This was the main source of Steve Cogswell's income. Far Away Holidays paid him only a nominal salary to be their Riviera representative. The side tours were his own enterprise and to the extent that he was able to sell them he compiled enough money to allow him to live comfortably through the season and then to take off for almost six months during the winter.

He had tours to Italy, tours to Grasse, the world perfume center, tours to the mountains, trips to the various islands off the coast, fishing trips and skin-diving outings. This particular week he had the bullfight at Nîmes, which was to take place in the well-preserved ruins of what had once been a Roman arena.

By the time he had finished in Menton, it was getting on into the day and he hurried back to Monte Carlo to contact as many as possible of the twenty-odd clients who were staying there. Some he was able to locate before lunch, which speeded things up.

Time was running out on him by the time he was finished. He hopped into the Citroën and headed for Nice, taking the fast Middle Corniche road, which was much quicker than the older route that bordered the sea. As usual, in passing through the town of Eze, he was taken aback, all over again, with the view from this eagle's nest of a town perched more than thirteen hundred feet above the sea.

In Nice, most of his clients were either still at their leisurely lunches or were sitting on the Ruhl terrace finishing things off with coffee and a brandy. Steve took just long enough to have a quick brandy himself, exchange a couple of fond words with Joseph, possibly the most popular bartender on the Riviera, and then went into his sales pitch again.

It was late afternoon before he pulled up before the office of Far Away Holidays in Monaco.

Elaine was getting her things together, preparatory to calling it a day. She gave him the messages which had accumulated since he'd left that morning, took a few notes, and then looked at him pertly. "Well, this is the day you make your donation to the Casino, isn't it? Should I get you the usual one hundred new francs from the cashbox?"

Steve Cogswell grinned sourly. Roulette was his weakness. He was self-disciplined enough, however, to realize he just wasn't in the category where he could throw money around. Consequently, he allowed himself to play every Saturday evening, when the stiffest part of his work week had ended.

He allowed himself a hundred new francs—roughly twenty dollars. If he lost that, it meant he didn't gamble again until next Saturday. If he won, and that was seldom enough, he allowed himself to play again, whenever he had free time during the week, until he had lost all his gains. Of course, he didn't *always* lose. In fact, he'd hit it good one time nearly two years ago and had wound up the evening with almost ten thousand francs. Happily, on that occasion he'd had the good sense to invest it the next day in the Citroën station wagon he now drove. It was just as well he did. His luck changed again that very night.

Elaine was opening the cashbox.

Steve said suddenly, "How much is in there?"

She looked up at him, "About a thousand new francs, Monsieur Cogswell."

"A couple of hundred dollars. Let me have it all."

She shrugged in typical Gallic fashion, but said nothing. He was the boss. It was his money. Luckily, Elaine Marimbert reflected, citizens of Monaco were not allowed to enter the Casino. That was one foolish dissipation that Prince Rainier didn't allow his people.

* * * *

Somebody waved to him from another automobile as he was parking in the Place du Casino. He frowned at first, not recognizing the vehicle, but then he realized it was Nadine Whiteley. She pulled up next to him and called, "How do you like the car?"

It was a practically new Simca convertible, and she seemed pleased with it. "I feel unpatriotic," Nadine said. "I've never driven anything smaller than my Pontiac before."

Steve leaned on the car door, on her side, and said, "Well, you don't have to be. This car is the product of an American manufacturer with a plant in France, so somebody in Detroit is making a profit. What're you doing?"

"Just driving about and enjoying the sights."

"Good. Come on into the Casino and bring me luck."

She looked up at the heavy, ornate building. "Is this the famous Monte Carlo Casino? I though it was a government building."

"Looks more like it at that, doesn't it?" he said, opening the door for her. "Actually, it's the oldest casino on the Riviera, first started back in 1856. By now it's on the ancient side, compared to the ones in Cannes and Nice, but it's become an institution."

He led her up the stone steps and into the elaborate, Victorian period lobby where he bought their admission, saying something jokingly over his shoulder about the incongruity of having to pay for the privilege of losing your money.

He changed his thousand francs into fifty-franc chips and led the way into the gaming room. "Don't forget," he told her. "Keep your fingers crossed for me. I've got to win five thousand dollars tonight."

She said, taking up his light mood, "I'd root for you, but I don't know anything about roulette except that the little ball goes round and round and finally sinks into one of those holes. Then the croupier rakes in everybody's money. This knowledgeability I gained from Hollywood movies."

"Mmmmm," Steve said glumly. "Well, that about sums it up."

They took their places at one of the wheels and he explained roulette. "That wheel has eighteen red holes, eighteen black, and one white, into which the ball can drop. On this green table, here, you place your bets. If you put your money on any single number and it comes up, you win thirty-five to one. If you place it on either red or black, odd or even, or above eighteen or below eighteen, it's called a *chance simple* and you win one for one. There's various others ways you can bet, such as a *cheval*—putting a chip between two numbers, then if either of them comes up you win seventeen to one."

"Very good," Nadine nodded. "There's just one more thing I'd like to know. How do you break the bank?"

Steve pretended to wince. "That I've never found out," he admitted.

"You mean you have no system?" she said chidingly.

"Oh, I've got a system all right. I've got several of them." He placed a bet on red. "This is called the *escargot* system."

"That means snail, doesn't it?"

"That's right. And that's because it goes so slow. However, it's comparatively safe. You bet one chip and continue betting one as long as you win. As soon as you lose, you write the number 1 on a piece of paper, like this, then stake two and continue as long as you lose. The moment you win again, you cross off your first number on the paper and you play three chips until you win again."

She was frowning in concentration at his explanation.

Steve said, "The advantage of this system is that even if you lose five bets and win five you'll still be five chips ahead. It's based on progression. Your luck has to be pretty bad to lose much."

Steve didn't lose. He won.

After about a half-hour of play, he looked into her face and chuckled. "By golly, I think you *are* bringing me luck. I'm going to switch to the *Tiers de Tout.*"

She'd had one set of fingers crossed and openly displayed for him thus far. Now she grinned back and crossed a pair on her other hand. "Let's go," she said. "What's the *Tiers de Tout*?"

Steve had divided his pile of chips into three equal stacks. Now he placed one of them on a *chance simple*.

"I'll show you how it works," he said. There was a faint sheen of sweat on his forehead. "It means the *third of everything* and you win fast—if you win. You play one third of your chips on a single bet. If you lose, you follow up with the two remaining thirds."

She blinked. "Then if you lose twice in a row, you're broke."

"That's right," he said. "If you win either bet, you divide your money again into three stacks and bet one of them. If your luck is with you—and here you are standing right next to me—you pile it up quickly."

The croupier grinned at Steve and said, *"Bonne chance, Monsieur Cogswell!"* Then to the rest of the players, *"Faites vos jeux. Rien ne va plus."*

Nadine frowned skeptically. "Why should he wish you good luck? Whose side is he on?"

Steve was concentrating on the spinning ivory ball as it hopped from one slot to another. He said, "Henri works for a salary. If I have good luck, I'll tip him. Obviously, he hopes I'll have good luck." Steve won and sighed satisfaction.

An hour later, his shirt was soaked with perspiration. Steve looked at her, the side of his mouth twitching slightly. "Look," he said, "let's go into the *Salle Privée.*"

She raised her eyebrows and he explained. "That's the inner room where the stakes are higher. You have to pay another admission—keeps the riffraff out. Usually, that means me, but tonight I'm out for blood."

He stuffed his chips into his pockets and they went down the long length of the public rooms to an ornate guarded door which led to smaller, more luxurious rooms beyond. Before resuming his play, he took her into the small bar that led off to the right. There were but six stools, and for a moment Steve hesitated when he saw one of them was occupied.

Then he said, "Hello, Conny," to the other. He was a dark-complected, heavy-set man. Now his thick eyebrows went up.

"Hello, Steve," he said. "How is your luck running?"

"Fine," Steve said evenly. "Nadine, may I introduce Mr. Constantine Kamiros? Conny is possibly my oldest friend here on the Riviera. Miss Whiteley."

The Greek tycoon got down from his stool and bent over her hand formally. "I must try and take you away from Mr. Cogswell," he said softly. "It is a game we play against each other."

Steve attempted a chuckle. "Not tonight, please, Conny. Miss Whiteley is my luck and I need her badly. I've decided to win five thousand dollars this evening."

"Indeed," the other said, his shaggy eyebrows high again. "You have picked a difficult method of acquiring such a round sum of money, Steve."

Steve shrugged. "Can't be as difficult as all that. Isn't gambling the manner in which you got started, Conny? And now you reputedly own half the Riviera."

The heavy-set Greek grunted deprecation. "I learned early, Steve, that to win at roulette you must stand on the opposite side of the table."

"Touché," Nadine laughed. "Heavens, are those One-Armed Bandits, over there? Excuse me, gentlemen."

Kamiros said, smiling thickly, "Miss Whiteley, your choice of game chills an old gambler's heart. There is no gambling action ever devised by man that gives the player so poor a percentage."

But she had gone to the long rows of slot machines that lined one wall of the bar.

The Greek turned back to Steve Cogswell. "Well, Steve?"

"It's a dirty trick, Conny."

"Indeed? My friend, look at yourself, and then look at me. How old are you? Thirty-three or so? Look at your physique and your lean, perhaps handsome, American face. Then look at me, Conny Kamiros. I am fifty-one and not too well preserved a fifty-one at that. Perhaps I spent too many of my earlier years sitting at the card tables, to get proper exercise. So today, when we are rivals for a beautiful woman, you present a considerably better, ah, front, than does Conny Kamiros."

"What's that got to do with collecting that loan on a week's notice? Besides, the girl is back in London now."

The Greek looked at him strangely. "We all have our egos, friend Steve. You strike a man's ego hard when you take his woman. Very well, you have your comparative youth, I have what everybody knows Constantine Kamiros has—money. In the conflict between two males for beautiful women, we must use what weapons we possess."

Steve said stiffly, "I'm sorry I upset you so much, Conny. I, too, in my time, have had my woman taken away from me by a supposed friend."

The Greek began to say something, but Steve spoke quickly. "I wasn't about to beg. Your point is well taken. I don't hold it against you, Conny, and I'll either dig up the five thousand or my property is yours. And now I had better round up my good luck charm, before she loses all her coins."

He turned to go.

Conny Kamiros began, "Steve…"

But Steve Cogswell walked away toward where Nadine was energetically pouring coins into two machines at onces. "Broke yet?" he asked her.

Her face was nearly as flushed as his became in the excitement of roulette. "Broke?" she said happily. "I've never seen machines with such a good percentage. You should see the terrible ones we have in the Country Club back home. I must be fifteen dollars ahead!"

Steve said, "You really are hot tonight. Let's not waste it on slot machines. Come on into the gaming rooms and you can place my bets for me. The *Tiers de Tout* system is going to get the work-out of its history."

It did. It was fully an hour later that Steve Cogswell, feeling physically limp, emotionally drained from the fast play, totaled up the stacks of chips and plaques before him.

He said hoarsely to Nadine, "Nearly thirty-five thousand new francs."

She whistled softly. "What's that in coin of the realm of Uncle Sam?"

"About seven thousand dollars."

"Heavens to Betsy," she said, awe-stricken. "When you came in here you were kidding about winning five thousand dollars. But you did it!"

He eyed the green-topped table, listening a moment to the croupier's chanted *Faites vos jeux*, and moistening his lips. "I'm hot. I suppose I should continue the play."

She looked at him from the side of her eyes. "Why did you want to win five thousand, Steve?"

He grimaced. "I owe it to Conny, in there."

She said, "I don't want to be a dominating female, old chap, but gambling being what it is, I suggest we march into the bar and throw Mr. Kamiros his filthy lucre."

But Constantine Kamiros was no longer in the bar, nor evidently elsewhere in the Casino. By the time Steve and Nadine had discovered that, Steve's playing ardor had left him. He cashed in his chips at the offices in front and was paid in five-hundred-franc notes, which he stuffed into his pocket.

"I can look Conny up tomorrow," he said. "Meanwhile, we're going to throw the biggest celebration the Côte d'Azur has seen for yea many years!"

"Mister," she said, matching his exuberance, "you talk me into it!"

They ate at La Bonne Auberge, on the main Nice-Cannes road, and Monsieur and Madame Baudoin themselves supervised their selection of traditional dishes of the cuisine of Provence and the Riviera, and the wines of Burgundy and Bordeaux.

Over their table passed bouillabaise, then rouget grilled with fennel, artichokes à la barigoule and Bohémienne de Provence, and finally the goat cheese of Banon with its wild thyme flavor.

At last, reeling with food, they took off for a tour of the Riviera's offerings in the way of night life.

The Candy Club in the Palais de la Méditerranée, in Nice; the Trocadero in Cannes with its *La Belle Epoque* décor; the Summer Sporting Club in Monaco; and finally the little *boîte* of Gordon Payant in Juan-les-Pins.

They wound up holding hands here in the candlelit bar as the American Negro folk singer strummed his guitar and in the hushed silence of the tiny place sang in French and English, Spanish and Italian, German and Russian. The songs of little people, of peasant and soldiers, of children and the old, of the lover and the loved.

After a song there was never applause. The jampacked room resounded intead to the snapping of fingers.

Nadine was puzzled until Steve explained. This little *boîte* was in a residential section of town. Neighbors had complained about the noise several years ago when Gordon Payant had first opened up. So the institution of snapping the fingers instead of applauding was inaugurated.

Payant spotted Steve and called over to him. "Any requests, Mr. Cogswell?"

Steve waved back. "How about *Little Boy, How Old Are You?*"

The singer's deep voice rendered the strange song with moving effect.

Little boy, how old are you?
Little boy, how old are you?
Why, sir, I'm only six years old.…

They returned finally in the early hours, sleepily, satisfied, the two of them. Steve Cogswell pulled the car into garages of the Pavilion Budapest and turned to her.

He hesitated, momentarily, before saying, "How'd you like to drop down to the trailer and have a nightcap?"

"Oh, is that your trailer near the beach? I can see it from the window of my room." She thought for a moment, only a moment, then said, "That sounds fine, Steve. Excuse the cliché, but I hate to see this night ever end."

The half-moon gave some light but Steve took her by the hand to lead her across the lawn and to the path that wandered down the cliffside to where his trailer was parked.

He felt a thickness in his throat. And she too knew what was ahead and an excitement was growing within her. This time would be different. This time she was calm and collected and knew what she was doing.

In the small living room of the trailer, he didn't even bother to switch on the lights. He turned to her and said huskily, "Nadine."

His arms slid around her and his lips mashed against hers. Pent-up passion flooded out to meet him, a decade of frustrated desire. As though widely experienced, her mouth opened hungrily and her tongue darted forth to meet his and to kindle flames that roared through them both.

They sank to the couch, still glued together, and his hands ran over the contours of her body, quickly becoming impatient of her restrictive clothing.

His hands, ultra-experienced, quickly darted to button and zipper, to clasp and elastic. They were both breathing heavily, urgently. Her own hands began to help his, to fumble with his clothing. Their minds were blank except to their passion, their need for relief from this frantic burning.

She was murmuring, over and over again, "Yes, yes, Oh, so good. Oh, yes. Please, yes. Oh, darling!"

And his voice was thick as he whispered endearments and admiration of her femininity. The swell of her rich, naked breasts, the softness of her woman's belly, the sweeping curve of waist and hips, the smoothness of her long thighs.

Deep within him he knew that all his worship of her tonight would sour by morning; and deep within him he hated himself for the fact. But there was no turning back. The urgency was all-conquering.

And then she suddenly squirmed, pressed her hands against his chest, her words of endearment and passion choked off. He was pressing down upon her.

"No," she gasped.

"Darling…" he muttered, unconscious of her changing reactions.

"Oh, no!" she said tightly. There was horror in her voice. She pushed at him. "I…no…don't…you can't…"

He stared at her, shaken with the suddenness of the reversal of her passion "What is it, darling? What's the matter? Aren't you ready?" He began pressing against her again.

The girl was rapidly descending into hysteria. Her eyes were wide—staring wide. With alarm, with actual terror. She clasped her hands to her naked breasts, trying to cover herself, and from her mouth came meaningless, gibberish.

"Uncle Nat! Don't do that… Oh, no, Uncle Nat… Oh, please don't. I'll tell father… Don't hurt me… No… Oh, no—"

Steve came to his feet, stood back. "What's the matter?" he all but snapped.

She rose from the couch. In a trice she had gathered her clothing. She scooted around him, like an animal fleeing a deadly foe.

He put out a hand to detain her—not aggressively.

But she avoided him, dodged and was through the trailer's screen door and gone.

He stared after her retreating figure, running hard for the rock stairway that led to the Pavilion Budapest above.

Stumbling her way along, half-clothed, sobbing, desperation sweeping her, Nadine's mind raced her despair.

Like always before. Like with Roger Stuart. Always the same. Uncle Nat's drunken face before her. His passion-flushed, drunken face. The pain, the fear, the horror. Like with Roger Stuart. Like with Gerald Silletoe.

CHAPTER THREE

Sunday, August 7th

Gerald Silletoe was seated in one of the two clients' chairs in the Far Away Holidays office when Steve Cogswell turned up in the morning. He was seated quietly, thumbing through some of the tourist literature which lay on the tiny table which centered the room.

Steve missed seeing him at first.

He said to Elaine Marimbert, before she could make with her usual *Bon jour*, "If there're any crises today, break them to me gently, honey bun. I don't know if I'm in a good humor or bad. I've been lucky in finance, unlucky in love."

Her pert face wrinkled with astonishment. "The great Don Steve, unlucky in love? *Incroyable!*" But then her delicately plucked eyebrows perked up. "You won at the Casino? Enough?"

He grinned at her. "Impossible, eh? But the answer is yes."

Elaine clucked her pleasure for him. She took a cable. "Only one crisis, this morning, and that's from London."

He read the cable quickly, groaned and closed his eyes. "My God! Ten extra clients next week and I have to find reservations for them by that time. The boss must think this is May, instead of August. You can't scare up first-class accommodations on the Côte d'Azur this time of the year on five days' notice.

"Well, we'll see what we can do. Maybe the contessa can pack in some of them. Meanwhile, get me Conny Kamiros on the phone, Elaine. Brother, has *he* got a surprise coming to him, the old louse."

Elaine Marimbert cleared her throat. "Monsieur Cogswell, this gentlemen has been waiting to see you."

Steve turned and confronted the other, who now came to his feet.

"I'm sorry," Steve said. "Didn't see you at all."

"It's all right," Silletoe said easily. "Could I talk to you alone?"

Steve looked at him. Obviously an American. Well dressed in the latest sort of thing you saw from Florida and southern California. However, there was a certain something missing in his squarely handsome face. What would you call it? Perhaps a something known as breeding. Snap judgment told Steve Cogswell that the man made a bad first impression—at least he did on Steve Cogswell.

Steve said to Elaine, "How about going over to the garage and making arrangements for the bus to Nîmes? There'll be thirty-seven of us in all. I imagine the big Renault will be best, if it's available."

"*Okéy*," Elaine said. She darted another quick look at Silletoe as she passed him on the way to the door.

When she was gone, Steve turned to the newcomer. "What can I do for you, Mr...."

"Silletoe," Gerald Silletoe said evenly, almost patiently. "I just arrived this morning. And I don't like something a...a friend told me."

Steve frowned, waiting for the other to get to the point.

Silletoe said very evenly, "I want you to stay the hell away from Nadine Whiteley, Buster."

Steve looked at him. "That's not quite the way to word it, is it?"

"That's exactly the way to word it, Buster."

"And why should I stay away from Miss Whiteley?"

"Because she's my fiancée, Buster, and I told you to."

"I don't like the tone of your voice, Mr. Silletoe. But besides that, I don't know Miss Whiteley well enough to have known she was engaged."

Inside, Steve was trying to fight off his growing irritation with this aggressive heavy. *Heavy* was the only term he could think of to apply to the other, who reminded him of nothing so much as a prosperous gangster type in a B movie. He did everything but speak from the side of his mouth.

"You know her too damn well," Silletoe said flatly. "I'm going to emphasize what I just told you, Cogswell."

He stepped forward so quickly that Steve had time neither to retreat nor erect defenses.

The heavier man shot his right hand forward, not doubled in a fist, but pointed spearlike. It jabbed with shocking force into the small area on the stomach wall just below the sternum—the solar plexus. Even a trained boxer can be knocked out, on occasion, with a blow to this point, even when delivered with a gloved hand.

Steve Cogswell was no boxer and the hand was not gloved. The room reeled and turned black. Steve felt another smashing blow to the side of his head, and then he was on the floor.

He came out of it how many moments later, he didn't know. Silletoe was nudging him less gently with the toe of his shoe. When he saw Steve shake his head in an attempt to achieve clarity, he said evenly, "Now I've warned you politely, Buster. Stay away from Nadine Whiteley. Next time I'll get rough."

He was gone before Steve had recovered to the point of coming to a sitting position and then to his feet.

He stumbled his way, nausea churning his stomach, to the small lavatory which was the only other room in the Far Away Holidays quarters besides the office. There he washed his face and otherwise cleaned himself up.

In spite of the pain which still racked his chest, he had to grimace ruefully at himself in the mirror. His luck with Nadine had certainly changed for the worse after she'd helped him win the money at the casino.

He couldn't figure Silletoe out. Nadine's fiancé? It didn't seem likely. And the man had said he'd just arrived that morning. How could he possibly have heard gossip rumors about Steve and Nadine so soon?

Not that it was any of his business, confound it. After that performance the girl put on last night, if he never saw her again it would be six months too soon. In the past five years he'd been with some far-out women, but he'd never gone through an experience like the one of last night in his trailer. And to top it all off, here her boy friend had turned up and half-killed him.

By the time Elaine had returned from the garage, Steve had brushed the dirt from his pants and light jacket to the point where he thought of himself as presentable.

She said, "I was able to get the Renault. It will be ready immediately."

Steve cleared his throat, "Fine," he said.

Elaine looked at him, cocking her head to one side. "It would have been more gentlemanly if he had taken off his ring," she murmured.

"What?"

"There's a small triangular cut on the side of your cheek, Monsieur."

Steve dabbed at it with his handkerchief, and scowled at her.

"The price of being a Casanova, no doubt," Elaine said snidely.

He ignored her. "Get Conny on the phone for me, Miss Marimbert," he said.

She marched around the desk, her hips swaying pertly, and dialed the number. She said, after a moment, "Mr Kamiros has gone off to Geneva for a couple of days, Monsieur Cogswell."

Steve growled, "Nick Lindos will probably do."

She spoke into the phone again, then looked up. "Mr. Lindos went with him, Monsieur."

Steve swore under his breath. "It's not important," he said. "Look, I'd better start rounding up the tourists for Nîmes. Thirty-six of them signed up for the bullfight. Some crazy American kid who's all the rage down in Spain this year is fighting. Probably get himself gored, the way things are going today, and then all the clients will put a beef in to London that I took them to a gruesome spectacle. Anyway, you stay here and hold down the fort."

"How about the night club tour tonight?"

"I'll have time to handle that, too. You figure on the tour over to Grasse tomorrow. And have a talk with Pierre Labby in the shop there. That crook is supposed to kick back to me ten percent of everything my clients spend for his perfume, and he's been holding out."

"*Okéy*," Elaine told him. She gave a sly snicker. "The bleeding has stopped, Monsieur Cogswell."

"Thanks," he snarled at her, as he went through the door.

* * * *

He had forgotten that Nadine Whiteley was one of the tourists who had signed up for the trip to Nîmes and the bullfight. He picked up his contingent at Menton, then at Monaco, and then looked at his list to remind himself whether or not any of the several clients who were staying at the Pavilion Budapest were on this tour. Yes, Nadine was, and a middle-aged Englishman named Farrell. He had the bus driver stop to collect them.

Actually, until now Steve hadn't had time to go back over the events of the night before, nor his episode with Silletoe that morning. Aside from a sense of outrage at the unprovoked and deliberate surprise attack, and a desire to meet the man under more satisfying circumstances, he hadn't analyzed his feelings.

Nadine and Farrell had been awaiting the bus, sitting in lawn chairs and discussing the bullfight to come. Neither of them had ever attended one. They came to their feet and were ready to mount into the vehicle almost as soon as it had stopped.

Steve had been seated alone in one of the double seats at the extreme front of the bus. Nadine hesitated, then took the place next to him.

Oh, oh, he thought. Another complaint. This was all he needed, somebody sore who'd send up a written complaint to John Brett-James in London. Steven Cogswell, his Riviera representative, was attempting to seduce the cash customers. Seduce, hell—she'd probably write that he'd attempted to rape her.

Steve directed the driver to head for the Ruhl Hotel in Nice, where they were to pick up the last contingent of tourists, and then settled back in his seat next to Nadine.

He began cautiously. "Miss Whiteley, I'm afraid that I was, uh, carried away last night. Probably too much celebrating. Particularly after you'd brought me so much luck. I'm afraid an apology—"

"Oh, no," she said. "Oh, please don't." Her voice was a whisper. In fact, there was almost a whimpering quality in it.

"But..."

"You're the one who deserves the apology," she said, her voice low and her eyes turned away from him.

He didn't know what to say.

Nadine continued agonizingly, "I...I don't know much about these things, but, well, I understand that it's very difficult for a man... I mean..." She was blushing now. "I mean it's very cruel to leave him under such circumstances."

Steve stared at her in amazement. Far from being angry at him, the girl was apologizing for stirring him up and then leaving.

He said, "Look, don't worry about that part of it. Let's start all over again, eh? Friends?" He put a hand out to be shaken. "Well forget it all."

She shook with him, her clasp tight. Now that she faced him, he could see the touch of tears in her eyes. *Damn, but she's pretty*, he thought.

They picked up the balance of the tourists in Nice and headed down the coast. The trip was a long one, 290 kilometers, some 175 miles, but happily the roads were good. They passed through Cannes and twenty-two kilometers further on reached Saint Raphael where they turned inland.

There was a speaker system in the bus and a hand mike up front, and from time to time Steve brought the attention of the group to this or that sight they were passing. Tourists tended to get restless on these long treks.

Ordinarily, he didn't run tours this far away from Nice, but the opportunity was too good to miss. Even after he'd paid for the bus and driver, for their lunch and for the bullfight tickets, he'd net well over a pound profit per tourist, more than a hundred dollars for the group.

They stopped briefly in Arles for an examination of the Roman and medieval ruins, and had a lunch based on bouillabaise at the Thévot, on the Rue du Forum.

Nadine and Steve had kept their conversation light and desultory thus far. There seemed to be an embarrassment—which both were conscious of and both attempting to shake off—between them.

He didn't know how to bring up the matter of Silletoe, nor even if he should, but finally it came out, just before they reached Nîmes. He blurted, "Your fiancé dropped into the office this morning."

Her face registered confusion. "Fiancé?"

"Mr. Silletoe."

"*Jerry Silletoe!* He's here? Why..."

It was his turn to be surprised "You didn't know?"

"But, that's impossible. He's back in New York." She looked at him strangely. "But why did you think he was my fiancé?"

Steve ran his hand along the side of his cheek, ruefully. "He let me know in a rather emphatic way."

She was still astonished. "I had no idea Jerry was in France, but certainly there is nothing between us. We...well, we had a slight attachment at one time."

"You don't have to explain to me," Steve said.

Nadine was slightly irritated. "I wasn't explaining to you. I'm just amazed. First, that he's here at all; second, that he claims to be engaged to me. Steve, I...I'd rather you didn't tell him where I'm staying. That is, if you haven't already."

Steve said drily, "I'm afraid a man of his determination won't have much trouble locating you."

The bus driver turned to Steve and said, *"Nous sommes ici, Monsieur Cogswell."*

They were entering Nîmes.

Steve came to his feet and took up the microphone to give a brief talk. He kept it light, grinning to take the sting out of some of his words. "Folks," he said, "you'll note there's quite a crowd. Bullfights aren't a common thing here in southern France and when a name fighter comes up from Spain, there's usually a turnout.

"The *corrida* is held in what is probably the best-preserved Roman ruin in Europe. This arena is where gladiators once fought to the death, and you might keep in mind that the bullfight is a direct descendant of the Roman meets. In short, it can sometimes be a bit gruesome to those who are squeamishly inclined, the ladies in particular.

"In fact, some might become distressed and wish to leave. What I'm building up to is that there are thirty-seven of us and when the fight is over we're going to have to get out quickly and start on the return trip. We can't afford to separate. We'll go as a group—all our seats are together—but if anyone leaves the group, be sure and note where we have parked the bus, and be there by the time the fights ends at about—" he looked at his watch— "five-thirty."

He grinned again. "With thirty-seven people, it's almost certain that someone will get the idea of wandering off for a beer or to see some sight, or do some window shopping. Please don't. We just don't have the time. Okay, here we are. I've got the tickets. Just follow me."

They filed out of the bus and Steve led them toward the ancient amphitheater. They'd hit it pretty well an the dot. He could hear the band inside playing a *pasa doble*.

Steve said out of the corner of his mouth, to Nadine, who was walking beside him, "In spite of that little talk, just watch. By the time we get back to the bus there'll be anywhere from two to eight of them missing."

She shot a look at him from the side of her eyes. "Then what happens?"

"I get a new ulcer trying to find them, but usually they're in the nearest café, or on the nearest shopping street." He added bitterly, "Tourists are like children. People who are probably perfectly normal in their own home town—responsible, respected citizens—go utterly vague as soon as they become tourists."

In spite of herself she had to laugh at him. "Don't forget, I'm one of your tourists," she said.

"Hardly an ordinary one," he said. Then, when she stiffened: "I didn't mean it that way."

* * * *

Their seats were in the first *tendidos*. Steve made a point of rejecting *barrera* seats for the double reason of expense and avoidance of having his tourists too near the more gruesome aspects of a *corrida*. He'd once had a woman splattered with blood, and the howl that had gone up from London, when she demanded her dress be replaced, had taught Steve a lesson—particularly when he himself had wound up with the bill.

The first *tendidos* were near enough. By the time Steve's party had arrived, several of their places had been appropriated by strangers who had evidently decided to move down from higher seats in the belief that these had remained unsold. Steve had to put pressure to bear through the ushers, to get all thirty-seven of his people into their reserved places.

There were few unsold seats that day. *El Americano*, all the rage down in Spain this year, was packing them in. The other two *novilleros*, one Spanish, one Mexican, Steve had never heard about, but the American boy had been getting a bit of publicity. Steve, who'd seen *corridas* in Spain, was anxious to see him fight.

They were coming in for the *paseo* now, all three of the matadors carrying their *monteras* in hand, an indication that this was their first fight in this ring this season. They and their *caudrillas* following them made a brave spectacle in their *trajes de lucas*. They faced the judge's box.

One of the tourist women hissed at Steve, "What are they doing now?"

"Saluting the judge," Steve said. "The equivalent of the Roman gladiators saying, 'Hail, Caesar. We who are about to die salute you!'"

"Good heavens," the woman said. "You don't really expect anybody to be hurt, do you? I thought...well, I read that here in France they have laws that prevent them from even killing the bull."

Steve said drily, "That's the trouble with laws, they're so easily broken. In France they're forbidden to kill the bulls and an impresario is fined a few hundred francs if he allows it to be done. However, that's what the crowd wants, so every fight the bulls are killed and the impresario is fined, and everybody is happy."

The *paseo* broke up, the ring servants, mules and picadors retreating back into the bowels of the arena and the *toreros* taking their places behind the *barrera* walls. A trumpet sounded.

A black bull exploded into the ring, dashed around for a moment, head high, searching for an enemy, his eyes unaccustomed to the glare of the afternoon sun. One of the colorfully clad *peónes* ran out, dragging his cape. The bull exploded after him.

Steve explained to the tourists seated in his immediate vicinity.

"The bull hooks at the cape, and the matador who is going to fight him, can see what horn he favors and other characteristics that might influence the later stages of the fight."

The *peón* escaped behind a funk hole just as the bull crashed into it.

Now one of the matadors stepped out, cape in hand. He stamped his foot and his call could be heard throughout the arena. "Huh, *toro!*"

The bull spun and headed for him.

"It's the American kid," Steve said. "Now watch. What he's doing now are called *verónicas*, one of the basic passes."

El Americano held the cape with both hands, slowly swept it before the bull. From this distance and at this angle, the horns seemed to come unbelievably close.

Nadine, seated next to Steve Cogswell, said something in her throat and her hand clutched Steve's thigh, unknowingly. He grinned. This wasn't the first time he'd had this experience. There is a sexual connotation in the viewing of the danger inherent in the *fiesta brava*. In his time, Steve Cogswell had been with women frigid to begin with, who couldn't wait for the end of the fight before wanting to return to the hotel—and to bed. It seemed to affect women in such wise even more than it did men.

The *torero* went through a series of passable *verónicas*, then did a *media-verónica*, swinging the cape around him and bringing the bull to a standstill, fixed. He turned his back and walked to the *barrera*.

The stands were roaring *olés*.

Steve shrugged. "He wasn't that good."

One of the tourists said to him, "Yeah? Well, I'd hate to be down there."

"So would I," Steve said mildly, "but I'm not a trained bull-fighter."

The other was argumentative. "Are you saying it's not danger-ous if you're a trained bullfighter?"

It wasn't Steve's job to antagonize the cash customers. How-ever, he said evenly, "It's dangerous but not so much as they'd have you believe. It doesn't begin to be as risky as, say, racing hot rods. I doubt if it's as dangerous as prize fighting."

The tourist, an irritating type, hooted his opinion of Steve's statement.

Steve said, "A name matador hasn't been killed since Manolete in 1947. How many men have died in automobile races since then? The Old Brickyard up in Indianapolis averages one man killed, each race each year; there isn't a bull ring in the world that aver-ages one dead *torero* a year. How many bulls does a matador finish off during his career? Two thousand or more. You figure that out percentage-wise and you see that in any given fight the chances against the bull are rather high."

"I still wouldn't want to be down there," the other muttered.

The picadors were giving the animal a brutal working over to the point where the more knowledgeable in the audience set up a cry of protest. A horse was thrown back against the *barrera* wall, the picador unseated.

From the side of his mouth, Steve whispered to Nadine, "Along about here the exodus starts."

"Exodus?" she said.

Two of the tourist contingency were on their feet. "I…I'm go-ing to have to leave," one said.

"Please return to the bus," Steve called after them.

El Americano and his colleagues in the ring below were per-forming *quites*—making passes with their capes that brought the bull away from the horses, after each lancing. The bull's back was pumping red blood where he had taken his wounds.

Two more of the tourists left, one holding her hand over her mouth.

Nadine said, "Does it get much worse than this?"

Steve said, "It always ends with the bull's death. How clean a kill the matador makes is dependent on his skill. It can get on the grim side."

The bugle blew and the horses withdrew to be replaced by the *banderilleros*.

"This is the part tyros usually like," Steve explained. "The danger, and what is being done, is obvious. You don't have to be an expert to understand what's going on."

A gaily clad *banderillero* dashed out, stood on tip-toe for a moment, citing the bull. It broke into a charge, and he ran toward it in a quarter-circle. Just before impact, he spun away, the two, yard-long darts which he'd held in his hands impacted in the bull's shoulders.

The crowd yelled its *olés* and another *banderillero* dashed forth.

"I suppose *that's* not dangerous?" Steve's debating opponent said, argumentatively.

"I suppose it is," Steve said, untruthfully. The danger of placing *banderillas* for a trained *torero*, he knew, was largely an optical illusion. However, he kept reminding himself, he wasn't here to fight with tourists.

El Americano didn't show up too well in the *faena*. The bull had been worn down by the picadors and *banderilleros* to a point where it was nearly dead on its feet. After two or three *pase naturals*, the matador dedicated the animal to a movie actress who was present, posed with the sword and then went in for the kill.

Either he didn't know his business, or the bull was a paragon of gristle and bone. *El Americano* made six attempts before the bull went to his knees and was finally finished off with a *puntilla* dagger.

There were shouts of *olé* throughout the arena, but four more of Steve's tourists were making their way to the exits, some of them talking disgustedly, one of them a bit green about the gills.

Steve said to Nadine, "Most of the rest will stick. You either rule out the *fiesta brava* the first time you ever see one, or you become a fan. Evidently this trip I've got about twenty-five fans. What do you think about it?"

Another bull was erupting into the ring below and a *peón* ran out to attract its attention.

"I don't know," Nadine said. "I think I'm fascinated more than anything else, but I don't know if I'd ever come to another one."

The bull nearly caught the running capeman, and she automatically clutched Steve's thigh again.

* * * *

It was dark by the time the tourist bus had returned to the Côte d'Azur. As predicted, two of the tourists had been absent when the rest returned to the vehicle following the fight. It took a full half-hour to locate them in the bar of one of the hotels. It was the couple who had first left the arena. By this time they were nicely plastered, and apologetic. They hadn't known the fight was already over.

Nadine had sat next to Steve again on their way back to the Riviera. They had talked, in fits and starts, for a time, then as the weariness of the long day overcame her, she wound up with her head on his shoulder and deep in sleep.

Steve looked down at her. It occurred to him that he was finding her attractive all over again, in spite of the happenings of the night before and in spite of his farcical experience with Silletoe.

That brought Silletoe back to his mind and Steve scowled into the darkness. What was the man's game? Evidently he intended to brook no rivalry for the American girl's affections. But from her account, Gerald Silletoe had no claims on her whatsoever. There was something here in the way of undercurrents. In spite of Steve Cogswell's desire to remain unconcerned, it was attracting his curiosity.

He dropped the tourists off at their respective hotels, and Nadine at the Pavilion Budapest and made his way to his trailer for a quick shower and change.

No rest for the wicked, nor the tourist representative, he told himself sourly. He had another batch of people tonight who wanted the night club tour of the Côte d'Azur. It would take him well into the morning and after the long day's drive, he was in no mood for it.

The night club tour was one of his most lucrative. He ran it every Sunday night, and usually had about forty of his people signed up. He'd visit three clubs, at each of which the group would have one free drink and see the floor show. He would then take them to Gordon Payant's bar, where they got another free drink and where they could stay as late as they wished, returning to their own hotels by taxi.

Steve was able to get a good rate from the clubs, where he paid a flat amount for each customer, no matter what was drunk, which might run from Coca-Cola to Champagne. The clubs knew that although the first drink was free, the tourists often bought a few more before the show was over. Also, they might return the next night if they liked the place. Steve charged a flat three pounds per person and netted almost half of that, even after paying for the rental of limousines to get the group about.

Tonight was misery. He could hardly keep his eyes open, after the day's grind. He tried to remember how much sleep he'd gotten in the past few nights. Precious little. He was going to have to crack down on himself, and particularly his night life and drinking. He wished that he'd let Elaine take over this tour, but then he'd wanted her to take the early morning group to Grasse, the perfume center, on the morrow.

Somehow, he managed to last until they reached Gordon Payant's place. He got his people seated, then went over to where the Negro singer was having a cigarette between performances.

The other grinned at him, his teeth large and white. "Man, you look beat."

"I am," Steve grumbled. "Is that an American cigarette? Let me bum one, will you?"

Payant shook out a Camel for him, and lit if off his own. They'd been friends for several years now, Steve being a folk song buff.

"Look," Steve said, "I must have a king-size bill with you by now. I haven't paid up for my tours for the past three weeks."

Payant shrugged carelessly. "You're good for it, Steve. I'll look it up in a day or so and send the tab to Elaine. You going to be at Carla's party?"

"Going to be?" Steve muttered. "I *was* at Carla's party, Thursday night."

Payant chuckled. "This is evidently a new one. Dave Shepherd was in earlier. He invited me. Late Tuesday afternoon."

"I know," Steve said. "Supposedly a cocktail party, but it usually goes on until morning, and nobody gets anything to eat except hors d'oeuvres."

"After a few of those drinks Shepherd mixes, nobody wants to eat," Payant said. He scowled at his friend. "What's the matter, Steve?"

Steve Cogswell's face had gone suddenly ashen. He put his

hand on Gordon Payant's arm. "Look, that couple just leaving. Going out the door."

Payant squinted his eyes against the gloom of the smoke-filled room, tried to make out the two at the far end of the bar. "What's the matter with them?"

They were gone. Steve knew that he'd never be able to squeeze through the crowded tables in time to find them before they disappeared on the streets outside.

He shook his head. "No," he said. "I'm just tired. It couldn't be."

"Couldn't be who?" Payant demanded. "Man, you sound like you been blasting pot."

"My former wife, Fay. And Mart Gunther."

CHAPTER FOUR

Monday, August 8th

Fay and Mart Gunther didn't show up at the office until early afternoon.

Steve had slept late himself, knowing that Elaine would be able to hold down the fort until it was time for her to take over the tour to Grasse at about eleven o'clock. He had slept until ten and then taken a quick dip with the contessa and Dave Shepherd.

That pair of perpetual partygoers were, as Gordon Payant had reported, planning a cocktail affair for the following day. Dave, who was splitting the expenses with Carla, was all for making it a theme party, with Morocco as the theme. Moroccan decorations, Moroccan hors d'oeuvres, Moroccan drinks.

"That's all I need," Steve told him. "Moroccan drinks. That hangover I got from your absinthe frappés is hardly over. My friends, please count me out."

"Ha!" the contessa, whose figure was never better to be appreciated than in a bikini, told him. "Carla has heard this many times. Count me out, this *loup-garou* of the Côte d'Azur says, but when the party begins, with the drinks and the girls, who is always flittering around?"

"Flittering around," Dave had giggled. "Now that's an apt way of putting it. What is a *loup-garou?* It sounds frightfully appealing."

Steve was scowling at Carla, whose face was impishly innocent.

"It means werewolf," he said. "I don't get the application to me."

"But Carla thinks it is perfectly obvious," the contessa said. "All day long our hard-working Mr. Cogswell dashes about chaperoning his tourists, a perfectly respectable man. But when night comes he turns into a wolf. And what does he do to all the pretty girls? He lays them."

Dave fluttered his hands to his ears. *"Please,"* he said. "I just can't stand to hear women using four-letter words."

Steve was laughing.

Carla said seriously, "You know, this is a very strange thing. I could never say, in Hungarian, the equivalent of your four-letter words. Never in the world in my own language. But in English, or French, it means nothing to me. Nothing at all."

Steve said, "Well, believe me, it can come as a shock, when an attractive, cultivated woman meets you and out come terms usually associated with the poetry on rest room walls." He laughed again.

Dave went back to the party. "I could whip up a batch of El Majoun, and then we could fake some dancing boys."

"El Majoun?" Carla said suspiciously.

"Dancing *boys?*" Steve said.

"What is this El Majoun?" Carla said. "Already Carla suspects she doesn't like it."

"What's wrong with dancing *girls?*" Steve demanded.

"Well, my dears," Dave fluttered. "We do want to be authentic, you know, if we have a Moroccan motif. El Majoun is hashish fudge. You take almonds, walnuts, raisins, and honey, and butter, and—"

"Hashish fudge!" Carla said accusingly. "Oh, no, you don't. I can see just how long Carla would remain in business when the word got to the police that she served hashish fudge at Pavilion Budapest parties."

Dave shrugged his shoulders prettily, as though there were no pleasing some people, and turned to Steve. "Hollywood to the contrary, dear boy, you don't have dancing girls in Moroccan night clubs, or anywhere else that they might be seen by Christian men. It would cause riots. Instead, they have the cutest boys ever, all done up in Moroccan women's clothing. My dears, it's quite a sight. The boys are trained from childhood. They're specially, ah, prepared." Dave giggled again. "You know, emasculated."

"Hell!" Steve said. "I can see I'm going to stay away from this party in droves."

The contessa said indignantly, "Ha, no dancing boys in my villa, Dave Shepherd. If we are that short of dancers, Carla will dance herself."

"Oh, you people have no real imagination," Dave said, in a huff.

Steve leered heavily at Carla Rossi, letting his eyes sweep up and down her figure. "Now we're getting somewhere," he said, his voice low with pretended sexiness. "How about the dance of the seven veils?"

She swatted him across his buttocks, jumped to her feet and headed for the water. *"Loup-garou,"* she said over her shoulder.

After his swim, Steve had driven into Monte Carlo in the Citroën station wagon, arriving in time to relieve Elaine at the office. Her tourist group consisted of only fifteen persons, and she was taking them in a small Fiat bus.

There was the usual mail, none of it important except one from the Far Away Holidays office in London. The extra number of tourists was to be eight, not ten. Steve grunted something under his breath about giving thanks for all small favors and thumbed his way through the balance of the morning's offerings.

There was a cable for Nadine Whiteley from New York. He remembered her saying something about taking a drive up into the mountain villages of Provence in her rented Simca, so there was no way of contacting her before evening. He put the cable into his inner jacket pocket.

He kept himself busy at paper work until lunch, then ate over at the grill in the Hotel de Paris. One of the advantages of this job, Steve was of the opinion, was the fact that his duties including eating at least once a week in each of the hotels where the Far Away Holidays vacationists were staying—on the house, of course. Supposedly he was keeping tabs on the quality of the food. It couldn't be better than at the grill.

Back in the office again, he took up where he had left off. Thank goodness, at least, that he was getting neither phoned complaints nor enraged tourists calling at the office today.

It was then that the door opened, and there were Fay and Martin Gunther.

"Hello, Steven," Fay said.

"Hi, Stevie," Mart said.

In five years, Mart Gunther had gone a bit more to weight. His jowls were heavier, his movements on the sluggish side.

But the years had done little to Fay—little more than to realize the promise of the less mature beauty of her youth. The soft mouth perhaps was a trace less delicate than in yesteryear, the breasts a trifle less arrogant, but ah, the long legs, the striking body, the grooming and easy grace of Fay. It was all there. She was still all Fay.

Steve said, heavily, "Then it was you last night. Yes, of course." He pushed back his chair and came to his feet and motioned to the customers' chairs. "Sit down, Fay, Gunther."

For a brief moment, Martin Gunther looked as though he were going to step forward to shake hands, but then the automatic gesture of the hand checked itself and after he had seated Fay he took the other chair, sinking into it with a sigh.

He's beginning to be a fat man, Steve thought dully. *He's only a couple of years or so older than I am.* He sat down again himself.

Fay leaned forward. "Oh, Steven, how are you?"

He looked at her. Her lips were slightly parted. When he was a young man, he remembered, they had all but driven him crazy with passion. He hadn't been very experienced when he'd married Fay. Lord knows, he hadn't.

He said evenly, "I'm fine, Fay. How have you been?"

She looked around the office and gestured. "But this place. Why, you were the third man in your class at M.I.T., Steven."

"I like it," he said flatly. "What a coincidence, our meeting here. Vacation?"

Mart Gunther cleared his throat. "It's not exactly a coincidence that we're here, Stevie…"

"The name is Mr. Cogswell," Steve said flatly.

"Oh, Steven," Fay said.

His eyes left the face of Mart Gunther, a face that was beginning to darken, and returned to her.

She leaned forward again. Her voice was artificial. "Steven, haven't five years healed the wounds? They tell us that time heals everything."

"Yes, so they tell us," Steve said.

"Steven, can't you see that it was the only thing that could happen? We weren't happy. We could never have been happy. We just…we just weren't meant for each other."

"I didn't know that."

Her words came faster. She said earnestly, "Steven, listen to me. Martin and I are happy."

"You're married, eh? I wasn't even sure we were divorced."

Martin Gunther said, "We couldn't get in touch with you. Nobody knew where you'd gone."

"You said it was no coincidence, your being here," Steve said.

Gunther said, "Look, we might as well lay it on the table. Stevie—" He twisted his mouth. "Mr. Cogswell, if you want it that way. We located you through a private detective."

Steve scowled at him. "Why go to the bother?"

Fay gushed, "Steve, I had to apologize to you."

"All right, Fay, you have." Steve looked back to Mart Gunther. "And is that what motivates *you?* Is that why you hired a detective agency to locate me?"

Gunther said doggedly, "Look, it's been five years and you haven't even dropped us a postcard."

Steve suddenly laughed. "What did you expect? Something with the Eiffel Tower on it and me writing *having a wonderful time?* Somehow I had gained the impression that we weren't exactly friends any longer."

Gunther said, impatience in his voice, "I was talking about the firm, not Fay and me as individuals."

"The firm! You mean Gunther & Cogswell is still in existence?" Steve laughed again. He was getting the damnedest feeling of a lack of reality in this whole thing.

Gunther said, "It hasn't been easy. But one way or the other, I've kept things going." He shrugged his shoulders. "I won't bore you with the details. Among other things, Fay had to take a job."

Steve said, "Well, evidently the Horatio Alger bit came true. You've finally got to the point of doing well enough that here you are, taking a holiday on the Riviera."

Gunther's voice was still dogged. "This isn't a vacation trip, Stevie. I keep telling you that. I've got a couple of new partners. Good men who want to come into the firm. But it's not fair to them, or to Fay and me, for you to be a fifty percent partner. They're going to put up not only their own training and abilities, but some money as well." Mart Gunther pulled a handkerchief from his pocket and wiped moisture from his forehead. It wasn't a particularly hot day.

Steve said, "So you want me to bow out."

"It's only fair. You haven't even been in the States for five years."

Steve didn't get part of this. He frowned and said, "Why didn't you just dissolve Gunther & Cogswell and start off all fresh with these new men?"

Gunther made a gesture with his two hands, palm upward. "For one thing, the firm has been going for almost seven years. It's established, no matter how poorly it's been going. We're known in the field. Our publicity and advertising has had *some* effect on potential customers."

"It would be so much easier for us, Steven," Fay injected.

Steve came suddenly to his feet. "Look," he said, "where are you staying?"

"At the Negresco, in Nice."

"Okay. Let me think about it. I don't mind telling you both that I'm confused. Besides that, this is the height of my busy season and I've got a lot on my mind. Let me think about it and I'll check back with you shortly."

"I don't know what there is to think about," Mart Gunther protested, lumbering to his own feet. "I'm not asking you to give anything away. We'll offer you a nominal sum for your interest."

"I still want to think about it," Steve said impatiently. "Frankly, this has come as a shock to me. I never expected to see either of you again."

He ushered them to the door, taking Fay's arm as he guided her. His hand tingled with the contact.

Fay!

* * * *

They were gone.

Steve Cogswell locked the office and walked over to the little bistro on the corner at Avenue Saint Michel.

The *fille de comptoir* nodded to him. "Monsieur Cogswell."

He took a stool. *"Une fine, Bette, s'il vous plaît,"* he said brusquely. *"Armagnac."*

The barmaid's eyebrows went up. Monsieur Cogswell, the American who worked with tourists from England, was usually on the pleasant and smiling side. In fact, Bette had long been of the opinion that she held a certain interest for him and that it was just a matter of time before he attempted to develop a relationship.

It was all right with Bette, she was available. In fact, she was anticipating. Now she shrugged and poured the brandy. Evidently, even Monsieur Cogswell had his bad days.

He knocked the brandy back, stiff-wristed.

"Encore, Bette," he told her.

At this time of day? Bette shrugged again and refilled the glass. As she turned to replace the bottle on the counter behind the bar, he reached out and stayed her.

Monsieur Cogswell was evidently really in a bad way today. She left the bottle before him, as he desired, and went off to fill an order for one of the *garçons* who were waiting tables out in front on the sidewalk.

Steve knocked back the second drink, waited only momentarily before pouring still another.

He was shocked to realize the extent to which Fay was still able to affect him. Five years! Five years and a hundred women ago. How many women had he bedded since last he had seen Fay? He had no idea. Women in France and women in Spain, brunettes in Italy and blondes in Denmark, prim girls in England and lusty wenches in Germany. A compulsion, he sourly admitted to himself. This continual need to prove wrong the things of which Fay had accused him.

He poured another drink, downed it, then suddenly got down from his stool, tossed a bill on the bar and turned away, striding quickly from the place.

Bette picked up the money and looked after him. At least Monsieur Cogswell had left a tip large enough to double the cost of the Armagnac.

He went back to the office, got the station wagon and drove to the Place du Casino, where he parked and headed on foot for the Hotel de Paris. He had in mind putting a little pressure on René to get reservations for the eight extra tourists that were turning up this coming Friday, but the hotel manager wasn't there.

Steve went into the hotel bar and had another double cognac.

He couldn't understand what the hell Fay saw in Mart Gunther. She was at the height of her feminine beauty. Gunther had let himself become a slob. If it was simply a matter of sex—and that had obviously been their original attraction—surely she could do better now. Steve had another double.

René still wasn't around. Steve walked back to his car and then stared across the street at the Casino. He brought out his wallet and considered the sheaf of bills there.

What the hell. Easy come, easy go. Unlucky in love, lucky in finance. He counted off the equivalent in francs of five thousand dollars and tucked that amount into a compartment of his large, French-style wallet and then made his way to the ornate entrance.

One of the housemen at the inner door smiled archly at him. "We have been expecting you back, Mr. Cogswell. Do you think your luck still holds tonight?"

Steve growled something at him and went on past to the bar. He was feeling the quickly consumed spirits now. What the hell, it's not every day your past comes back and confronts you—and you find it's not past at all.

What the hell, let's face it. He was still in love with Fay.

He ordered another double and a moment later stared down into the empty glass. He couldn't remember drinking it. He looked at the bartender suspiciously.

"Another one, sir?" that worthy said in English.

"Yeah, damn it," Steve said accusingly. He'd never noticed before, but Edouard was obviously a bastard. Well, the bastard could just see how much of a tip he'd get. What was the big idea?

He was at the roulette table.

The hell with this system stuff. If the number was going to come up, it'd come up. It was all luck. No system was any better than any other. The fact that this damn Casino was still here and in business after a century of wise guys figuring out systems showed that nothing worked. If anything worked, the Casino would be broke, wouldn't it?

The croupier said, anxiously, *"Ca va, Monsieur Cogswell?"*

"I'm all right, Henri," Steve slurred. "Spin her." The fog rolled in.

When it rolled out, he was back at the bar. He hadn't remembered leaving the wheel. He felt in his pockets. There didn't seem to be any chips. He couldn't remember if he'd lost them all, or cashed them in, or what.

That called for a drink. When you got silly enough that you didn't know what you did with your chips, you'd better start stopping, or stop starting, or however you wanted to put it, and start doing some serious drinking, or you'd lose all your money.

Suddenly he was afraid to look into his wallet to see if he'd gone into the five thousand he'd reserved for paying off his bet to Conny Kamiros. That was a dirty trick Conny had pulled on him, just for the sake of soothing a ruffled ego. But, damn it, had he been so tight that he'd gambled away the five thousand, too? He didn't think so but he didn't dare look.

He ordered another drink, noticing that Edouard was frowning worriedly at him. Good old Edouard, one of the best bartenders in Monaco. One of the best? What the hell. *The* best. He decided to leave a good-sized tip for his old pal Edouard. Along in here the fog rolled in again.

When the fog rolled out, he was in some bistro that he didn't remember ever having seen before. He shook his head and made a mental note never to see it again. It was a hole-in-the-wall.

His vision cleared. He slurred, "Why, hello, Nadine. I didn't see you."

She laughed. "Didn't see me? Good heavens, for the past half-hour you've been telling me how you used to pack up into Kings Canyon National Park with somebody named Old Mart and fish for trout."

He shook his head again. "Hell, I feel awful. What time is it?"

She looked at her watch. "About ten."

"How long—I mean, what happened? I'm afraid I'm a little tight."

"A *little* tight. I'd hate to see you really hang one on," she laughed at him. "I saw your car parked outside, about an hour ago, and looked in to see if you were here. I wanted to ask your advice on where I should drive tomorrow. You seemed to be a…bit under the weather, so I thought I'd rally round."

He looked at her for a moment. "Thanks," he said gruffly. "I guess I ought to be getting to bed. Would you mind driving me home? I think I'd better leave my car here."

"Let's go, pal," she said lightly.

* * * *

It was the same, or almost the same, as it had been the first time.

They had got Steve a couple of cups of black coffee and then, on the way back to the trailer in her Simca convertible, they'd put the top down and he'd let the cool touch of the Mediterranean night air wash over him.

He also remembered the cable that had come that morning and passed it to her and she'd put it away in her bag to be read when there was light. He had also checked his wallet, and found to his relief that the five thousand was intact.

There had been a strange simplicity in the way they had walked together down to the trailer. An air of inevitability, that seemed to dominate everything.

She hesitated only momentarily at the trailer door.

"Are you all right now?" she said.

"Of course. Stone sober." There was a husky quality in his voice. She was ethereal in her beauty in the moonlight which struck her in such manner that her light blouse seemed not exactly transparent but actually nonexistent. It seemed as though her full breasts were bared.

She said then, a touch of indignity in her voice, "Then why in the world did you allow yourself to get that tight? You don't seem to be the lush type."

He grinned at her, wanly. "And you don't seem to be the scolding mother type. I suppose I was being stupid, but I saw a ghost today."

"A ghost?"

"My former wife. She and her new husband are staying in Nice." He held the trailer door open and she entered and sat down on the small couch.

"I see," Nadine said. She looked down at her hands, folded in her lap. "Should it be as upsetting as all that? Are you still in love with her, Steve?" Then she said quickly, "No, don't answer that, of course."

He sat down next to her and there was an electric quality in the air. A touch of lightning. Nadine drew in her breath and felt her woman's body respond to his animal maleness. Guided as though by an alien power without her, she reached forth her hand. Her eyes closed and she touched his thigh as she had at the bullfight in Nîmes—but this time consciously.

She tensed, and grasped him intimately. It was an instinctive, almost involuntary gesture and already he was ready for her.

She felt her senses swooning away as his eager hands moved on her, trembling, exploring. He forgot the other night. He forgot everything except this woman's body, the treasures of the darkness her thighs framed.

Her blouse was gone, her breasts, the nipples warm cherry stones, proud, erect and demanding. She moaned when he took one in his lips.

"Darling, it's so good," she whispered. "Don't wait any more.

Oh, Steve, don't make me wait any longer...." Her voice fell away into incoherence.

Steve had never seen a woman in this extreme of need. Far away in his conscious mind, he was surprised, even, in a way, compassionate.

But that was his conscious mind, and a different reality. His current self was in a blind passion, possibly as strong as her own. He fumbled with his clothes, the sound of belt buckle and zipper loud in the silence of the night.

"Oh, quick," she moaned.

He descended upon her waiting, yielding body. Now, this was it. This was the moment of truth, of glory. He pressed hard, ready to possess her completely.

Suddenly she dissolved into a screaming, pounding, squirming, scratching, she cat. Her small body, perhaps seventy-five pounds lighter than his own, abruptly displayed a strength beyond him.

In pure shock, he scrambled to his feet and stumbled back two or three steps, standing nude before her, to the rear of the trailer's small living room.

Mewling like a terrified animal, Nadine grasped up blouse and skirt, and blindly darted for the light which marked the open but screened trailer door, suited to the summer heat and the occasional Riviera mosquito.

The screen banged open and then shut, behind her.

"Sonofabitch!" Steve blurted.

It took him several full minutes to control himself to the point where he stopped shaking, trembling with emotional crisis.

He looked down upon himself ruefully. "I must be losing my grip," he muttered.

Then, partly in a return to the drunkenness and despair from which she had rescued him, he growled, "I've got to do something about that. One way or the other."

He dressed and made his way up the path to the Pavilion Budapest. Nadine had disappeared. Probably, he decided viciously, cowering in her bed, behind a locked door. To one side, he seemed to see some movement. Was that a man's figure, silhouetted over there? No, of course not, at this time of night.

He looked up at the contessa's villa. There was a light in Carla's bedroom window. He wondered, in his present condition, what response he would get if he knocked on her door. But then he shook his head. His relationship with Carla Rossi had been a long one and a friendly one. And she had been right, the other morning. It they became intimate just once, the friendship would be over. He knew himself that well. And evidently she did, too.

His own car was parked back there in front of the bistro where Nadine had found him, but that was no problem. She had left her keys in the Simca. The emergency was of her own making. She could hardly begrudge him the use of her vehicle to get into town and find some kind of relief, both physical and psychic.

* * * *

He picked the tart up in the Place Massena and followed her to her small hotel on the Avenue de la Victoire. She spoke English, as tarts are apt to do in Nice, the center of British tourism in southern France. She spoke English and had evidently worked out a system of cutting the time afforded a customer by arousing him with words before they ever got to her room.

She told Steve Cogswell, as they walked along the Avenue, just what it was she was willing to do for him. And her words were graphic. The darkness of sex was again upon him by the time they reached her room.

It was a sad room, a drab room, as so often are the dens of those who sell human flesh. He sat on the bed and looked at her, his face expressionless. Already some of it was going out of him.

"Love me, honey?" she smiled, her fingers going to the clasps at the side of her garish, tight, tart's dress.

He didn't answer her, but his face was flushed. She knew all the signs. Her mind was clicking away at business details, even as she disrobed provocatively. This one had been drinking. Drinking too much, which was sometimes bad. But he was an American and, hence, rich.

She would ask double her regular price and then he would probably tip her besides. It would probably take longer than usual, if he'd been drinking as much as she suspected, but then the amount of his "little gift" to her would more than make up for it.

The dress fell away and she smiled again. She wore nothing beneath except black silken panties and she hooked her thumbs in these and slowly, deliberately pressed down. She smiled into his eyes. "Like me?"

He still said nothing. He just sat and watched, his face flat.

She was worried. Was this one too drunk to perform? Sometimes when that happened, the customer got mad, and then anything might develop. She hoped there would be no noise. This hotel was not a bad base of operations and she didn't want to be ordered from it.

She kicked her shoes away and literally nude now crossed over to him, taking short, provocative steps to arouse him the quicker. *Zut!* this one was cold.

She stood before him, hands on hips. "You like it?" she said, her voice low.

Steve bit out, as though irritated, "Evidently not."

He was surprised at himself. The girl was cute, and young. They were seldom this young, even on the Côte d'Azur. Her body was still firm, and evidently comparatively unused. And, heavens knew, she was willing.

She sat down beside him and fondled him with an expert hand. "Perhaps you are too drunk, *hein?*"

"No, that's not it," Steve growled. Actually, he didn't know what was wrong. He'd come here, coldly and deliberately. Now something was wrong.

The girl leaned closer to his ear. She whispered, "I am a French girl, you know."

"No," he said brusquely. "I don't want that." He came to his feet and scowled down at her. He began to say something, an excuse to leave, but she stood, too, and took him by the hand and led him to the bureau. There was a wicked wisdom in the way she looked at him from the side of her eyes.

"Ah, I know your kind," she murmured. "You will see. It will cost more, but you are willing to pay. No?"

He didn't know what she was talking about until she opened one of the drawers. Inside were three or four whips of various design. Behind him, she opened the closet door. "Or perhaps some of these," she said, her voice heavy with urgency.

In the closet were fantastically high-heeled shoes and women's leather boots that laced almost to the knee. Rubber clothing of various types. Leather clothing, both male and female. Ropes and cords.

His gorge rose.

She said throatily, "I will do anything Monsieur desires—for a price, Monsieur." She added, "Or do you wish me to do it to you?"

A sort of impotent rage swept him. He fumbled in his pockets for money, brought out a fistful of bills and silver, tossed them on the bed and, pushing her angrily and brutally aside, pulled open the door and stumbled into the corridor beyond.

Too overcome with conflicting emotions to wait for the elevator, he walked, almost ran, down the stairs. He crossed the dingy lobby in what seemed to be no more than a dozen strides and emerged on the street. It took him a long moment to remember where he had parked the Simca.

He didn't remember, later, the drive from Nice to the Pavilion Budapest, a distance of three or four miles. He pulled into the parking area, and garages, and left the car in the spot where Nadine Whiteley had parked it earlier in the evening. He left the key in it, as she had, and started to return to the trailer.

The alcohol was gone from him now, but he was exhausted with the aftermath of both the drinking and the emotional tensions he had been through the last twelve hours. He didn't even see the hulking shadow which detached itself from a deeper shadow. The first he knew of the presence of the other was the crushing blow that hit him full in the belly.

He caved forward, in nausea and shock, and the second blow, a brutal uppercut, smashed into his face. He began to reel backward, but the other was upon him.

The blackness rolled over him. Idiotically, the last thought that went through his brain was, *After all this I'll be in no shape tomorrow to attend that party of Carla Rossi's....*

CHAPTER FIVE

Tuesday, August 9th

Carla Rossi was bending over him, shaking his shoulder frantically, her voice shrill with concern.

"Steve, Steve, what has happened to you? Carla looked out the window, and here you are on the ground."

He tried to return to life and reality. It was dawn. His jaw felt broken and there was still nausea in his belly. As poorly as his mind was functioning he was able to think, wryly, *What am I suffering from most, that sock in the stomach or pure hangover?*

He sat up and felt his jaw, waggled it back and forth. He looked up at the contessa. She was dressed in negligee, nightgown and bedroom slippers. For the sake of the usual banter they carried on between themselves, he tried to whistle and found he couldn't; his face was too swollen.

Steve said, "I had just parked the car. Somebody was hiding, somewhere. He managed to knock me out before I even so much as saw him."

She stooped and picked something up, recognized it and handed it to him. It was his wallet.

Steve came to his feet and inspected it. It was devoid of money—both the five thousand dollars' worth of new francs that he had held in reserve for Conny Kamiros, and whatever he might have had left after his night on the town. He groaned to express both his physical and mental anguish.

Carla said worriedly, "Come into the kitchen, Steve. We'll clean you up, get some coffee into you. Then Carla will phone the police. Did you lose much?"

"At least twenty-five thousand francs," he said bitterly. He decided that the jaw wasn't broken but, Christ, it hurt.

She clucked in sympathy. "About fifty dollars in your American money."

He grunted in self-deprecation. "Twenty-five thousand *new francs*, Carla. Five thousand dollars."

She stopped and stared at him, her eyes wide. "Carla doesn't understand. What were you doing with so much money, Steve?"

"Like an ass, I was carrying it around waiting for Conny to come back from Switzerland, so I could pay him what I owed him. I won it Saturday night at the Casino."

They were in the kitchen of the villa. It was still early morning. The contessa was the earliest riser at the Pavilion Budapest. Even after an evening-long party, she was always up and around before the servants. She took a clean towel from a drawer, moistened it at the sink and dabbed at his face, clucking her tongue in sympathy as she worked.

The contessa moaned softly, "Steve, Steve, five thousand dollars. So much money! And I have heard the rumors going around. Conny has insisted that you repay him a loan he made you."

Steve Cogswell grunted disgustedly. He imagined the story was being circulated by the gossip route all up and down the coast. Even his supposed friends were probably secretly pleased by his come-uppance dished out by Conny Kamiros. Steve's romantic activities weren't always well received either by husbands or lovers of the Riviera's more attractive glamour girls or by those women themselves whom he had bedded and then deserted.

"Carla will phone the police immediately," the contessa said. "It is a matter for the police. With luck, perhaps they will find this villain before the day is out, eh?"

"No, wait," Steve said.

"Why this wait? The sooner they begin to look for this *apache...*"

"I don't know why," Steve said, and he didn't. "But something is wrong here."

"Something is wrong, yes. You have had twenty-five thousand new francs stolen. But it is for the police. Carla will..."

He was shaking his head, stubbornly now. Steve said, "Whoever slugged me not only knew I had the money, but also knew where I lived and must have had some idea when I'd return. It wasn't just some stray thug. I've got to think."

He'd been sitting on a chair as she administered to his cuts and bruises. Now he came to his feet and approached the small mirror that hung above the large double sink. He touched a cut on his face thoughtfully. Hardly had that cut from Jerry Silletoe's blow of the other morning healed up, but he had this new one.

Steve's eyes narrowed. How had Elaine described that nick Sunday morning? *A small triangular cut*, she had said, And so was this one. Silletoe's ring must have a strange setting. Or, for that matter, possibly he deliberately so mutilated anyone he struck. It wasn't beyond the man's obvious ego to mark his victims.

Steve said, "What time does Miss Whiteley usually come down for her breakfast?"

Carla frowned at him. "She is up early. Usually she swims, then goes off for long drives. Carla seldom sees her except at meal-time. This is a very nice American girl, Steve."

"I know. How early is early?"

"She should be down soon. Which reminds me, where is Annette? These servants!"

Steve said, "I'm going down and try to freshen up with a swim and get some clean clothes. I can see Nadine later. I'll see you later, too, Carla."

"You are sure you do not want Carla to phone the police?"

"Yeah, sure, but thanks." He started for the door.

She hesitated. "Steve."

He turned with a slight frown of impatience. "Yes?"

Her impish face was serious. "Steve, Carla has known you for nearly five years now. At first you were like a madman. Drink and women, drink and women. But then, what happened?"

Steve said nothing, frowning.

"I suppose the money was gone, eh? At any rate, the old Steve began to change. He secured a job, began to dress more carefully, was never seen any more reeling along the streets, unshaven. After a time the job became better—because he worked at it—and it became necessary for him to open a little office. And then hire that nice Marimbert girl, Elaine, for an assistant. And then he acquired a station wagon to help the work, and after a while a very pleasant little—what do you call them—caravan—"

"House trailer," Steve grunted, wondering what she was building up to, and impatient with it.

"Yes. So the new Steve has his nice little bachelor's trailer and his car and his office, and things go much better for him. Carla likes this new Steve better than she likes the old one." For a moment, the pixie quality that was Carla showed through again. "And she liked the old Steve fairly well."

"What are you getting at, Carla?" Steve said, self-conscious.

"I would not like to see the old Steve return," the contessa said. "Now listen to me, Steve Cogswell, Carla has in this house many paintings. Conte Rossi loved them. My husband loved them very much, but they are only paintings."

"Well?" Steve said.

She shrugged, "Only one of those gaudy-looking Matisse paintings, Steve, would bring much more than five thousand dollars. You could repay me any time. And then Conny would not have you—how do you say it?—over a barrel."

He put his hands on her shoulders and looked into her face. "You aren't the worst guy in the world, Carla."

"Ha! You wolf, only answer my question. This is no time for flattery."

Steve shook his head. "I've known you, Carla, when there wasn't too much food in this overgrown villa of yours. But it was the old count's love of his final years, and practically the only property left when he died. You didn't sell it, and you didn't sell a single one of his Picassos or Matisses. You're not going to do it now just to bail me out of a silly situation I brought on myself."

"But, Steve, Carla thinks…"

He chucked her under the chin, then bent down quickly and kissed her on the lips. Thanks just the same."

Carla stepped back, her hands on her hips and a skeptical look on her elfin face. "Ha," she said, "that is the first time you have every kissed Carla, Monsieur *Loup-garou*, and your breath smells like the bottom of a sour wine vat. However, the offer still stands and a painting is only a painting."

"And a principle is a principle," Steve said. "You've held onto those works through thick and thin, and I'm in favor of your continuing to hang on."

He left and went on down to the trailer.

As he started coffee on the buta gas stove, he went back over his scene with the contessa. It had never occurred to him before that Carla Rossi might be in love with him. Their relationship had always been on the lightest of levels. But now he had to consider whether or not that was other than Carla might have liked it.

She was still an attractive woman, one of the most attractive women he had ever known. And she was a *good* woman, in all connotations of that word. Any man who took up with Carla Rossi, either as his mistress or his wife, would get full measure. However, Steve grimaced, this was a complication he didn't want to face, at least for the moment.

While the coffee cooked, he stripped and got into bathing trunks. He made a dash for the beach and plunged into the warmness of the Mediterranean. He swam briskly until he was sure the coffee would be done, then hustled back. He still felt lousy, but at least better than before.

He poured a cup of coffee, leaving it black, and sipped away at it while cooking half a dozen strips of bacon in the electric skillet. When they were nearly done, he dropped two eggs into the pan, swearing as he managed to break both yolks. Okay, so he'd have scrambled eggs. He stirred them up, adding salt and pepper.

The sight of the food nauseated him, but he knew he was going to have to eat it. He had a lot to do today. Thank heavens there weren't any tours that he'd have to go on personally.

Steve got the hot food down, one way or the other, and three cups of coffee. Then he washed his face again, noting the bruises and swollen areas and the still evident cut, and dressed himself.

By the time he had returned to the villa, Nadine Whiteley was seated in the breakfast room. Her face looked almost as drawn as his own, he decided. What kind of a wringer did this girl put herself through?

He stood above her at the table and said, "Mind if I sit down?"

She looked up at him, quickly. "Oh, Steve…I…"

"Please, not again," he said gruffly. "I don't need an apology. You already went through that routine. If I was foolish enough to get myself into the same position all over again, it's my own fault."

She flushed and looked into her plate.

He took the chair across the small table. "It was something else I wanted to discuss with you."

"Something else?" She took up her coffee cup, but held it without sipping, as though trying to find occupation for her hands.

"This Gerald Silletoe, your former fiancé."

Her face stiffened and her voice went strained. "Gerald Silletoe, as I've told you before, was never my fiancé. But what—what can your possible interest…?" She broke it off and then said, with some dignity, "You read my cable."

He didn't understand. "I haven't the slightest interest in your cable, Miss Whiteley. All I want to know is something about this Silletoe guy. I have reason to believe that he might have attacked and robbed me last night."

Now her eyes were wide. She stared at him for a long moment. Finally, she took up her bag from the chair next to her, opened it and brought forth the cable in question. She handed it to him, wordlessly.

He looked at her for a questioning minute, not getting it, and then looked down at the message.

> GERALD SILLETOE ALIAS JERRY SILL HAS EVIDENTLY FOLLOWED YOU TO EUROPE STOP I PERSONALLY TOOK RESPONSIBILITY OF INVESTIGATING STOP POLICE RECORD VERY BAD STOP YOUR FRIENDS HERE ARE WORRIED STOP PLEASE RETURN SOONEST
>
> WILLIAM UPDEGRAFF

Nadine said tightly, "Bill Updegraff is my plant manager and one of my family's oldest and closest friends. The town from which I come is small and close-knit. From the first, Bill and various others were opposed to my going with Jerry. But, of course, they couldn't say anything. I'm of age and I'm a Whiteley. Whiteleys can do no wrong in Samara."

"You knew this guy was a grifter?"

"Grifter?"

"A crook, a gangster," Steve said impatiently.

She shook her head. "No. I just knew him as—well, to me, as a rather thrilling man from New York, so different from the local boys."

"I'll bet," Steve said wryly.

Nadine flushed again. She stirred her egg with a fork. "I don't know a great deal about men," she admitted, defensively.

"So I've discovered," Steve said.

She tightened her mouth as though holding back tears. "I… I'm sorry Steve. It's all my fault. I can't tell you about it."

"We've been through all that," Steve said brusquely. "This is something else. Sunday morning this Silletoe character came to the office and warned me to stay away from you. Then, before I had the slightest indication that he was doing any more than shooting off his mouth he slugged me—expertly, I might say—leaving a cut on my face very similar to this one now." Steve touched the nick with his forefinger. "The Sunday morning one healed, but I acquired this last night while being robbed of five thousand dollars.

I didn't see my assailant, but, particularly in view of that cable, I have a sneaking suspicion who it was."

"Good heavens!" Nadine exclaimed. "But how would Jerry know you had the money, or where he could find you, or…"

He explained, impatiently again. "If he knew Sunday morning that I'd been spending time with you, it means that either he or an accomplice has been following either you or me, or both of us. So he would probably know about my winnings at the Casino. If they followed me around last night, they probably would have seen me flashing my bankroll as I pub-crawled the Riviera, making a fool of myself. Look, Nadine, are you very wealthy?"

"Well, yes. I suppose I am."

"Then that gives us his motivation for following you here. Evidently you led this Silletoe guy on far enough that he thought he had a chance of marrying you."

Nadine had a beautiful ability to flush in embarrassment, a characteristic rapidly disappearing in American womanhood. She said, her voice so low as to be hardly heard, "Well, yes…"

He stared at her for a moment, comprehension just beginning to dawn. "You mean, he went through that same fantastic experience I have on two occasions now?"

Her blush was furious, but she tightened her lips and nodded.

"No wonder he's sore."

Nadine said, "He attempted to get in touch with me yesterday, but I was gone. Then, last night, he phoned. He was very urgent, very demanding. I told him I didn't want to see him, but he insisted. He said he was coming here this afternoon and I'd have to talk to him. He—he frightens me now, Steve."

"Well," Steve said, "at least you'll have plenty of help if you need it. Carla's giving a party this afternoon. And I'll be able to talk to him too. I can use a little conversation with that laddy-buck." Steve stood up. "I've got to get into town. I'll see you later, Miss Whiteley."

"Nadine," she said.

"Of course," Steve said. He turned and left.

* * * *

Exhaustion was beginning to catch up with Steve Cogswell, but there were things he had to do. From Carla's little office on the ground floor near the villa's main entrance, he called a cab and had it drive him to where he'd left the Citroën the night before. Then he drove into Monaco and to the Far Away Holidays offices.

Elaine looked up at his entry and winced.

Steve growled impatiently, "No cracks, please, Miss Marimbert."

But she ignored him to chirp, "More of the wages of Casanova, Monsieur Cogswell?"

This time he was more definite. "Shut up," he growled. "What's on the agenda today?"

She checked the desk calendar. "The boat trip out to the Iles de Lérins to see the nudist colony, and to Sainte Marguérite to see where the Man in the Iron Mask was imprisoned. We have twenty-five signed up for that this week."

Steve said, "Not important, anyway. We shop those tours out. We don't get enough to hire boats of our own. What else today, Elaine?"

"No crises. Nothing except routine, Monsieur Cogswell. You're a bit behind in your paper work. And here's a cable from London. Two of the regular flight have canceled their reservations. That means that the number of new reservations we have to find is only six extra instead of eight."

"That's good," Steve grunted. "Look, Elaine, you hold down the fort for the rest of today. I've got something to do."

She said, her voice minus its usual pert quality, "I saw Monsieur Kamiros walking along the street as I came to work this morning. He has evidently returned from Switzerland."

He closed his eyes, in pain. "Oh, great," he said. "What day is it, Elaine?"

"Tuesday."

"Another three or four days to go," he muttered. "Oh, great."

She looked after him when he had left, and then twisted her shoulders in Gallic fashion. Never a dull moment when you worked for an American. But at least he didn't pinch a girl's behind every time she walked past. In the back of her mind, Elaine added to that, *unfortunately*.

Steve Cogswell drove back to the Pavilion Budapest but instead of leaving his car in the regular parking area, he drove down to the gardner's cottage and the trailer nearby.

He didn't take the time to undress. He blacked out on the living room's couch and sleep reached up and engulfed him.

* * * *

In his dream, a hulking man the size of Buddy Baer but with the face of Jerry Silletoe was cutting him to ribbons. The other wore on his right hand an enormous set of brass knucks. He would grasp Steve Cogswell by the lapels of his sport coat with his left hand and then crash the brass knucks into his face, repeating endlessly, "Take that, Buster. Take that, Buster."

Steve could neither break away nor accumulate enough strength to mount a counterattack. He became aware that the vicious weapon on the other's fist was so constructed that each time he was hit, a new triangular scar was cut into his face. The thought came to his mind, *I'll look like hamburger before he's satisfied.*

The blows became less vicious and his attacker stopped saying, "Take that, Buster," and said instead, "Hey, Steve, wake up. Wake up, Steve, old boy. The party can't do without you."

Sleep rolled back. Steve said, "Ugh?"

"I brought you a drink, old boy."

"Go away," Steve said. "I've had a drink."

"This is another one. Dave Shepherd says it's a drink the Riffs make from raisins up in Atlas Mountains. Tastes like a mixture of port and glue."

"Well, tell Dave where he can squirt it. I've had the last of his concoctions ever." Steve Cogswell looked through the screen door at his visitor. "Hello, Bob, haven't seen you around lately."

It was only afternoon, but Bob Blakewell had an alcoholic slur. Come to think of it, Steve couldn't remember Blakewell at any time of day or night when he didn't have an alcoholic slur.

Bob said, "Oh, I've been here and there, old chap. Having a few drinks between drinks. Listen, do you know a Miss Whiteley? American girl. How do you Americans say it? Built like a brick outbuilding."

"That's not exactly how we say it," Steve said, running his tongue around the inside of his mouth. "Come on in, Bob. What about Miss Whiteley?"

The other entered, and slumped into one of the two armchairs. He was a man of possibly forty, his hair going quickly, his face red with the broken veins of the alcoholic. His face held a pallor seldom seen on the Côte d'Azur. He carried two glasses, one of them full, one nearly empty. He put the full one on the cocktail table next to Steve's couch.

"This one Dave sent down to you," he said. Then: "I thought I was doing all right with Miss Whiteley, plying her with strong spirits and all that sort of thing, but then some new bloke came in and she asked me to find you if I could and ask you to come up. Then she took off, like the devil was after her."

Steve swung his legs quickly to the floor and came erect. "Be right with you," he said, heading for the shower. He still felt shaky.

"It's a long time between drinks," Bob said accusingly.

"Drink that one Dave sent me," Steve said over his shoulder. "I don't want it."

Bob shuddered. "Neither do I," he said plaintively, "but any port in a storm." He brightened. "Did you hear that, old boy? Any port in a storm. I made a joke. You know, port, port wine."

"I heard it," Steve said grimly. He threw off his clothes, showered quickly, and dressed in fresh clothes, making a mental note to take some of his things to the laundry and cleaners. Then together they returned to the Pavilion Budapest, where the party was in full swing.

A cocktail party is a cocktail party whether it be in Far Cry, Nebraska, Sydney, Australia, or Beaulieu on the French Riviera. Guests stood about, glasses in hand, and chattered banalities at each other. Smoke eddied. Servants slipped around with trays of delicately flavored, expensive food, offering the hors d'oeuvres to palates so sandpapered with gin and smoke that such items as caviar and *paté de foie gras* became tasteless.

The contessa, being the contessa, had once revolted against this state of affairs and had offered her guests, along with the usual tasties, a plate of salted orange pits. Somewhat taken aback when they were accepted without comment, she had cut up a desk blotter into small squares and covered them each attractively with mayonnaise. They, too, went into the bottomless pit of the cocktail party appetite, without causing a stir.

There seemed to be about sixty persons present, about par for the course at one of the contessa's shindigs. The usual crowd of the French wealthy, American and British expatriates, a dozen assorted homosexuals, a writer or two, an artist or two, several of the highest-paid courtesans on the Riviera, several titled refugees of the type that spent most of their time going from party to party in order to eat. Steve saw no signs of Nadine.

Just so as not to be conspicuous, he went over to the bar and said, *"Un verre de Coca-Cola, Jean, s'il vous plaît."*

"Coca-Cola? Pour vous, Monsieur Cogswell?"

"No comments, damn it! Just give me the Coca-Cola."

He took the drink and stopped a moment at a group where Dick MacFarlane, the well-known British artist, was telling one of his inevitable jokes. He listened for a moment, caught the drift of the story, which was familiar to him, and moved on.

He stopped long enough to say hello to one of his Far Away Holidays clients whom he vaguely remembered as being a Mr. Kovac. He asked the usual questions about accommodations and whether or not the vacation was going along all right.

Mr. Kovac said it was going fine. They sure did things different here, didn't they?

"How do you mean?" Steve said vaguely. He was looking about the crowded room, still trying to search out Nadine. He hoped she hadn't gone off somewhere alone with Silletoe.

"Well, for instance, who's that big buck nigger over there?"

"I beg your pardon?"

"Over there, the one talking to that Rumanian princess or whatever she's supposed to be."

Steve said stiffly, "That's Gordan Payant. He has a night club nearby. Gordon's probably the outstanding folk singer in Europe."

"Well, if he's got so much on the ball why isn't he back in the States making important money?"

Steve said, very evenly, "Probably one reason is because Gordon's got two children and he wants them to be able to get a decent schooling. He happens to be a very good friend of mine."

"Hey, well, don't get me wrong. I don't have no prejudices."

"Of course," Steve said. "Well, excuse me, Mr. Kovac."

Carla shrilled something to him across the room and he swiveled his way through the press toward her.

Dave caught him by the arm for a moment and chattered, "Steve, dear boy, isn't it a perfectly lovely party?"

Steve grunted and said, "Where's all the Moroccan motif you were going to have?"

Dave giggled archly. "Well, in trying to dig up some nice lads to act as dancing boys, I got side-tracked and—"

"Never mind," Steve said, "tell me sometime when I'm not so prone to nausea. See you later, Dave. Carla wants something or other."

As he got nearer, he saw Gerald Silletoe standing next to the diminutive Carla Rossi. The burly American's face was dark and he was obviously just short of being in a rage.

The contessa, by the looks of things, had been needling him, and the contessa was an old hand at aristocratic needling.

She said to Steve now, "What does one do in your country with gate crashers, Steve?"

Silletoe said heavily, "I am not a gate crasher. I came to see Miss Whiteley."

Carla arched her eyebrows at Steve. "You see? But that sweet Nadine Whiteley does not wish to see him. What does one do, Steve?"

"You keep out of this, Buster," Silletoe snapped.

Steve said softly, "In this particular case, we might try phoning Interpol, Contessa."

She patted him on the arm. "Carla is sure you will handle it, Steve." And she swept away.

Steve faced Silletoe.

The other growled contemptuously, "What's this Interpol, Buster?"

"In your profession, I'm surprised you don't know," Steve said evenly. "It's short for International Police. Over here the police co-operate closely. For instance, if somebody dropped the word to the French *agents de police* that an American with a record was operating on the Riviera, they'd pick him up like a shot. If he tried to move over to Italy, the Italians would be waiting at the border. So would the British, the Belgians, or wherever he might want to go. I suggest you leave Miss Whiteley alone, Silletoe."

"There's no charge against me over here, Buster. I'm here as a tourist."

Steve said, "You'd be surprised how easily they can dig up a charge, these French police. They don't like tourists with long records. Besides, we have a charge. One that involves some five thousand dollars that was stolen from me last night."

There was amusement in Silletoe's eyes behind the surface anger.

"Buster, I don't know what you're talking about. But I've got an idea you'd have a hard time convincing the local John Laws you ever had five grand." He let his eyes go up and down Steve's attire, on the face of it, clothing that had cost a fraction of his own. "Where would a lousy tourist agent get that kind of dough?"

Steve said, low in his throat, "Maybe we better step out into the garden, Silletoe."

The other belched sudden laughter. "That'd be something, wouldn't it? Take a look at yourself, Buster. Your hands are shaking from boozing, your face is swollen from the last time somebody clipped you." He squinted at Steve Cogswell, in mock humor. "And I've got an idea your stomach still aches from the last time you ran into a real *man*. Don't be silly, Buster. You don't want to go out into the garden with me. An amateur should never fool around with an old pro at his own game."

What enraged Steve Cogswell was that he knew the other was right. On top of everything else, Jerry Silletoe outweighed him a good twenty pounds. But above all, he, Steve Cogswell, was still sick from hangover and the physical beating he'd taken the night before.

Silletoe snapped, "Now listen. You tell Miss Whiteley I'll be back here tomorrow afternoon. I've got something to show her. Something she'll be better off seeing. If she doesn't let me talk to her, the folks back in Samara are going to have some awful big changes in their opinions of the Whiteley family." He spun on his heel and clumped angrily through the French windows leading onto the lawn and was gone.

Steve Cogswell looked after him. He was beginning to wonder whether or not his own personal problems were quite up to those of Nadine Whiteley.

CHAPTER SIX

Wednesday, August 10th

Nadine had simply not understood what it was that Jerry Silletoe could be threatening her with. After the American grifter had left the contessa's party, Steve had found her and given her a rundown on what Silletoe had said. She was disturbed, but uncomprehending. Steve had advised her to talk to the man—in the safety of Carla Rossi's villa, and with Carla in easy earshot. Nothing could be lost by that, he'd counseled her.

Steve had then returned to the party, but only for a matter of moments and to call out greetings to Gordon Payant and other particular friends.

For the first time in years, this sort of get-together irritated him more than anything else—the gossip, the dirty jokes, the continual flirtation between male and female, both of whom were usually already married but far from being above a bit of extramarital dalliance. Silletoe's words about his physical shape and his being a boozer rankled him, but he had enough insight to realize their validity. *Face it man, you're a boozer—a lush and a woman chaser. Even scum like Jerry Silletoe is in a position to be contemptuous of you.*

The afternoon was well along by then. Steve had driven into Beaulieu, had a sizable dinner of *bourride* and *pieds el paquets* without the customary wine, and then returned to the trailer. He had a brisk evening swim and then returned to his bed. He hadn't framed it completely in his mind as yet, but he already had a germ of idea, and was working up a campaign.

In the morning he had almost completely recovered from both hangover and beating. He went through his usual routine, stressing a heavy breakfast and then took off for Monaco.

Early though he was, Elaine had already opened the office.

"Bon jour, Monsieur Cogswell," she told him, pertly.

"Okay, okay," he growled at her. "Get it out of your system. Let's hear a few wise cracks, then we can go to work."

Her eyes were wide in innocence. "But I didn't say a word, Monsieur Cogswell."

"Which is almost a dirty crack on its own," he said, grinning at her. "Listen, Elaine, get on the phone and locate a Mr. or Mrs.—either will do—Gunther, staying at the Negresco in Nice. Say that I'd like to see them soonest."

She began dialing. "You wish to speak to one of them?"

"Not on the phone. Just as soon as they can make it here. When they show up, find some excuse to leave for ten or fifteen minutes, will you, Elaine?"

"I can go over to the tourist office to see if there are any special events for next week's group."

Elaine made the date, and then she and Steve submerged themselves in the paper work in which he was falling behind this week. A dozen bills to be paid to night clubs, bus rental agencies, boat rental agencies, restaurants, and beach concessions where the Far Away Holidays people had privileges.

There were two letters from the London office, eating him out because of this complaint or that, about par for the course. Steve figured on somewhere between one and five beefs per week.

The phone rang and it was from one of the hotel managers. He was indignant. Two of Steve's clients who had represented themselves as brothers who wished to share a room evidently weren't brothers. Or, at least, if they were there was some strange incestuous relationship between them as well.

The manager explained, with true Gallic tolerance, that he did not mind two gentlemen who had unique ideas about sexual mores, but the occupants of the neighboring rooms were protesting against the noise and the sobs and cries that issued from room Number 69.

Steve placated him as best he could, promised he'd speak stiffly to the two offenders, and put down his phone with a sigh.

"These English," he grumbled. "Probably a couple of the most conservative people in their home town, scoutmasters, prominent church laymen. So they come all the way down here to do their version of living it up."

"I beg your pardon?" Elaine said.

"Nothing," he said. "You are much too young to know about

such things."

"Ha!" Elaine said.

The door was open for the coolness and he didn't notice the presence of Fay and Mart Gunther until Gunther cleared his voice and said, "Stevie—uh, Mr. Cogswell."

Elaine looked up and said, "I'll have to run over to the National Tourist Office, Monsieur."

Steve said to her, "Okay, Elaine," and then to Fay and Mart, "Sit down, please."

When Elaine was gone and everyone settled, Steve came to the point. "You wanted to buy me out, the other day. What did you have in mind in the way of payment?"

Mart squirmed grossly in his chair, his lower lip went out in a pout that made him look childish. "Well, not a great deal, Stevie. More like a token."

Steve looked at Fay. Fay the cool and self-possessed. She was dressed, as always, so as to look like a million. She'd always had that ability. Even when their fortunes had been at the lowest ebb, Fay had managed to look as though she'd never known what it was to stint on clothing. Now she crossed silken legs. "It's more a favor than anything else, Steven," she murmured.

It took an effort for Steve to say to her, "I don't believe I owe you two any favors." He looked back to Mart Gunther. "But I do need five thousand dollars."

"Five thousand," Mart sputtered. "I was thinking in terms of something like five hundred. Enough to make it worth signing the papers. But—good God, man, I didn't come here to be held up."

Steve was impatient. "Listen, if it's worth your while to hire a detective to locate me, and for the two of you to trek all the way over here, then five thousand dollars can't make that much difference to you and these new partners. That's approximately the amount I put into the firm in the first place."

Mart rubbed his chubby hand over his pouting mouth. "That original five thousand disappeared a long time ago, Stevie."

Steve Cogswell said nothing. He couldn't keep his eyes from Fay—from her lips, her body, the cunning turn of her ankles. His memory of her was so perfect that even now it took no effort whatsoever to picture her as he'd seen her so often in the privacy of their bedroom.

Fay had always slept nude, even in the winter months. It had been his pleasure to rub her back for her, and she'd responded, kitten-like. Fay had loved to have her back rubbed.

Mart Gunther brought his open hand down on a heavy knee in decision. "All right, we can probably swing it."

Steve said, "It only makes sense to me if I can have the money by the end of this week."

"But it's already Wednesday!"

"I know. And I need the money by Saturday morning, at the latest. Otherwise, it stops making too much difference to me, and I think I'd be inclined to say let Gunther & Cogswell fold—I don't want my name on the firm."

"I'll have to send some cables, make some phone calls, get hold of a lawyer who knows American law."

Steve said, "Then I suggest you go down to the American Consulate in Marseille. They'll put you onto somebody. I'll sign whatever you have drawn up, but I'll have to have that money in some negotiable form by Saturday morning."

"It's a bargain," Mart said, coming to his feet. He strode forward and held out his hand for a shake.

Steve looked down at it, then looked up into Mart's eyes and shook his head. "Come around as soon as you get your papers to be signed, and the five thousand. And if you'll excuse me now, Gunther, I'm busy."

* * * *

He finished off his correspondence with Elaine's assistance, took care of three or four other chores which were strictly routine, then left her at the office and headed for the Casino, walking for the exercise. He went down Boulevard Princess Charlotte to Avenue Saint Michel and then along the Boulingrins to the Place du Casino.

By this time it was open, although the clientele was limited largely to elderly women, highly painted, drably dressed in the finery of yesteryear. More than one, he knew, was here gambling for her day's expenses—her rent, her food, possibly her daily alcohol need. If she lost, she went without.

He had no difficulty in finding the croupier at the roulette wheel at which he'd been so lucky the past Saturday night. The other nodded to him and smiled. Steve had left him a notable tip on that occasion.

There were only two or three players at the wheel. Steve said, "Henri, could I talk to you for a few minutes?"

"Certainement, Monsieur Cogswell," the croupier said. He must have touched a button with his foot, or in some other manner signaled one of the prowling, inconspicuous housemen. This husky, discreetly garbed employee stepped quickly to Henri's side, his eyebrows up in inquiry.

Henri muttered something to him and the other took over his croupier's stick. "In the bar, Monsieur Cogswell?" Henri said politely.

"That's fine."

In the bar, they both took coffee. The croupier because of house rules, Cogswell because he was off the hard stuff for a while. Until he'd settled matters with Silletoe, he told himself.

They took their coffee to a table, and Steve came immediately to the point. "You remember my winning the other night?"

The other nodded. "Your luck was excellent."

"It came to some thirty-five thousand new francs."

The other pursed his lips. "Very excellent indeed, Monsieur."

Steve leaned forward. "The thing is, Henri, I was robbed of almost the full amount and I'm trying to find a way of proving the man who did it was responsible. One thing I've got to do is have evidence I had such a sum."

Henri was sympathetic. But what could he do?

"You could testify that I'd won that amount."

Henri shrugged hugely and regretfully. "I only know you won at my table, how much I am not sure. Nor do I know that you didn't lose it at some other table, or even in some other casino later that night. These things are unfortunate, Monsieur Cogswell, and I would enjoy doing you the favor, but my employers take a very bad view of Casino employees getting into legal matters. It brings unfortunate publicity."

Steve sank back in his seat. Actually, it was the answer he'd expected.

"If there is nothing else?"

Steve said, "One other thing. Those housemen who wander around. Do you know which one was in the vicinity of your table on Monday night, when I got so tight here?"

Henri considered, smoothing his hairline of a mustache with a thumbnail. "They circulate, you know, but Georg concentrates on my wheel, as a rule. I believe, in fact, he spoke to you Monday."

"Georg?"

"Georg Herzog. Possibly you have never noticed him. Part of the job is to remain inconspicuous. Georg is particularly efficient."

"Herzog? Sounds like a German."

"A former Nazi paratrooper, so I understand," Henri said expressionlessly. Steve knew that the croupier had been a French resistance fighter, several times decorated.

"I wonder if I could talk to him."

Henri came to his feet. "I'll send him in."

Georg Herzog did ring a bell, now that Steve Cogswell saw him. When the big, quiet-spoken German approached his table, Steve stood up and shook hands. The other palmed the hundred new franc note tip without change of expression. He drew up a chair and said, "Henri suggested you might from me some information want, Herr Cogswell."

"You know my name?"

The German shrugged. "I have seen you around for several years. In my position, we get to know the regulars."

"Monday night…" Steve began.

Georg said uncomfortably, "The reason I spoke to you Monday, Herr Cogswell, was beyond my usual call of duty. However, I have seen the gentleman's type before, and, of course, they at the Casino are not welcome. The least bit out of line, and the management so informs them."

Steve let air whistle from between his teeth. "The gentleman?" he said.

"The one I warned you about, Herr Cogswell."

Steve leaned forward again. He suddenly craved a drink, but he suppressed the desire. He said, "Listen, Georg, I'd had a bit too much that night, as you probably noticed. Tell me about this… gentleman."

Georg ran a finger down a faint scar along his jawline. He said carefully, "If you will pardon me, Herr Cogswell, you were making little effort to disguise the fact that your wallet contained a considerable sheaf of high-denomination banknotes. And that you, yourself, were a bit, uh, tipsy you Americans say?"

"I was that," Steve nodded. "I didn't know I was showing off my newly acquired wealth." His voice held self-deprecation.

The German shifted heavy shoulders and smiled without humor. "It is with me when I am in my cups the same. As I say, we have seen the type before. He was watching you, in just such a way. I spoke to you very briefly in warning."

"And what did I say?"

"I am afraid, Herr Cogswell, that you were too far gone to understand."

"I see. Could you describe this man?"

Georg Herzog's memory was perfect. So was his description of Jerry Silletoe. He wound up by revealing that the other had left the Casino only a moment or so after Steve.

Steve's voice had overtones of excitement now. "Could you testify to that? To the police?"

The German's bushy eyebrows rose. "Testify what, Herr Cogswell? That this man looked at your money in envy? I do not think my Casino employers would appreciate my going to the police with such a story."

Steve relaxed. "No, of course not. Damn it, I have nothing at all in the way of proof. Well, thanks a lot, Georg. I appreciate it."

Herzog looked at him speculatively. He said slowly and heavily, "Herr Cogswell, this man is your enemy, huh?"

"Yes," Steve said simply.

The German nodded. "Your face it shows you have been assaulted, huh?"

Steve touched the tiny scar on his cheek, and his jaw still felt swollen.

The German said, "Herr Cogswell, how long has it been since you have fought with a man in a serious fight?"

Steve thought back. "A couple of bar brawls a few years ago. Otherwise, not since I was a kid, I suppose. In modern life, you don't do much in the way of fist fighting."

"Of course not. Few men do—except in wartime. And what did you do when you had your bar brawls, invite the other gentleman back into the alley, and then the two of you put up your hands in Marquis of Queensbury fashion and flail away at each other? And if one was knocked down, stand politely back until he got up again?"

There was sarcasm in the ex-Nazi paratrooper's voice, and Steve flushed, but he said, "That's about it, I suppose. The same way we fought in school."

The German nodded. "I have this to tell you, Herr Cogswell.

That is not the fashion this enemy of yours will fight. I tell you again, I have seen his type before. He is a professional, Herr Cogswell. As I am a professional. If you and I were to fight seriously, right now, Herr Cogswell, I could kill you with my hands within a single minute."

Steve was taken aback. He realized that he didn't doubt the other's word.

The German continued heavily, "Herr Cogswell, you are raised a gentleman. You do not understand fighting. There is no gentlemen when there is fighting. There is only destroy or be destroyed. Sometimes there is only kill or be killed."

"Yeah," Steve said blankly.

The German looked at the blunt ends of his fingertips. "Perhaps you are in need of hired assistance, Herr Cogswell."

Steve thought about it. He shook his head. "Thanks, Georg, but my ego has taken enough of a beating these past few days. I don't think there'd be much left of it if I started buying protection against a man who isn't that much bigger than I am."

* * * *

At the Pavilion Budapest, in his conversation with Nadine Whiteley, Jerry Silletoe made it clear how they stood.

Nadine received him in the library, the door open and Carla Rossi obviously hovering not too far out of earshot of ordinary conversation. Carla had taken a shine to the obviously confused Nadine, and she was going to be sure nothing happened to the American girl under the roof of her villa.

They sat in the library, facing each other, in armchairs, and Silletoe made his pitch.

His voice kept the gentlemanly tone he'd cultivated over the years, particularly after he had reached the point where he could climb out of the gutters of Brooklyn. He said, "Nadine, you know I love you, that I've wanted to marry you, all along."

She made a gesture of negation with her hand. "Please, Jerry."

"What the matter?"

"Whatever little there was between us is over now."

"No," he said. "It's just beginning, Nadine."

"Jerry," she said patiently, "my plant manager, Bill Updegraff—do you remember him?"

"He didn't like me from the first."

"He didn't trust you from the first, Jerry. In fact, he evidently hired someone to investigate you."

Jerry Silletoe's eyes narrowed.

Nadine said wearily, "He found out about your—your career, Jerry."

"Look, Nadine," he said, "that's all in the past. But our marriage is the future."

She shook her head. "That's impossible, Jerry. I was taken up with you for a short time. But everything ended that night in Samara."

He put his hand into the inner pocket of his sport jacket and emerged with a large envelope which he handed over to her. "I'm going to make this blunt, darling. You need me. I need you. I'm willing to do anything to bring you around. Anything at all. Suppose, for instance, these photographs were circulated in Samara. You're the last of the Whiteley family, aren't you? How long have the Whiteleys been the pride of Samara?"

She didn't understand him. Frowning, she took the two photos from the envelope. They were unbelievably clear and detailed. She was in the process of fleeing Steve Cogswell's trailer, all but completely nude, her clothes grasped in one hand. The second photo must have been taken immediately afterward. She was in this, too, her face perfectly clear and identifiable; through the door of the trailer could be seen Steve Cogswell, also nude, his masculinity completely obvious.

Nadine stared in horror. "But…but it was dark. It was night."

Silletoe said drily, "The art of photography has progressed, darling."

"But there was no flash."

"Infrared flash. The human eye doesn't see it, but the film emulsion does."

In a frenzy, she tore the photos to shreds.

"I have the negatives," he said.

She continued to stare at him in horror. "One minute you tell me you love me, and the next you threaten to display these horrible pictures in my home town. You're…you're terrible."

He was shaking his head. "I know best, Nadine. You need me. You need marriage. Some way I've got to bring that home to you. Even if I have to threaten you to do it."

"You're insane!"

He was shaking his head emphatically. "You need a man, Nadine. You know perfectly well what those photos prove. They prove that the same thing that happened to us in Samara, that night in the front room of your house, happened the other night in the trailer. You need a man—but you're afraid. All right, marry me and I'll...I'll see that you get one. A real man, not a pip-squeak like that Cogswell."

She brought her arms closer to her body, in an attempt to control her involuntary shuddering. She said, her voice so low as hardly to be heard, "What you're saying is that once we were married you'd rape me."

Jerry Silletoe put a hand forward and laid it on her knee. "That's not the way to put it. You'd soon fit into a normal married life. Haven't I proved how much I love you?"

"By taking blackmailing pictures of me!"

He said patiently, "I knew from the first we were meant for each other, Nadine. When you came over here to Europe, I had you followed by a friend. By the time I got here, he already reported you going out with that lush, Cogswell. I realized I had to take measures, particularly since you're upset these days and don't really know your own mind. I admit I followed you and took those pictures. I needed something to impress you and bring home the reality of the situation."

Nadine's mind spun. She was emotionally empty. Perhaps Jerry was right, at that. If she married him, the situation would have to be brought to a head. He was strong, determined, forceful. Handing her affairs and herself over to Jerry Silletoe might end this perpetual drain on her emotional resources.

She brought both of her hands up to her mouth. "I don't know. I don't know," she said.

A new voice intruded upon them. "Everything all right?" Carla Rossi said brightly.

"Everything's fine," Silletoe growled. "Just leave us alone."

The contessa put her arm around the girl's shoulders. "You seem tired, my dear."

"Yes," Nadine said. "Yes, I am. I—I have to think. I must think."

Jerry Silletoe came to his feet, still glaring at Carla. "I'll go and make plane reservations," he said. "I'll take everything over. Don't worry about a thing, darling. Get a good night's rest and I'll come for you tomorrow."

After he was gone, Carla looked at the girl worriedly. "Carla doesn't want to put her nose in your business, but are you sure that you know what you are doing with that man?"

"I don't know. I don't know."

Carla said, "I think perhaps before you make an important decision about this man, you should discuss it with someone who Carla thinks likes you very much, eh?"

Nadine looked up at her, confused. "Someone who likes me very much? Here, in France?"

The contessa said, her face gently impish, "Carla has seen on the Côte d'Azur much of romance in the past twenty years, eh? Carla thinks someone who likes you very much is your countryman, Steve Cogswell."

CHAPTER SEVEN

Thursday, August 11th

Steve Cogswell was coming to the end of one tourist week, the beginning of the next. Tomorrow his usual contingent, sixty-seven in number, would be incoming, plus six extras. In spite, of Elaine's efforts, thus far they'd found no accommodations for the six. Every first-class hotel on the Riviera seemed packed. The boss should have known better than to have sold the extra package tours. What did he think Cogswell was, a hotel builder?

He had an inspiration toward noon.

"Listen, Elaine, phone Luigi Bertolini at the Royal Hotel in San Remo. Perhaps he's got some vacant rooms."

"San Remo? But, Monsieur Cogswell, that's in Italy."

"What difference does it make? It's only about eight miles from here, and they've got every facility on the Italian Riviera that we have on the French. If this home office saddles us with six more tourists than we have reservations for, they'll have to figure out some way of paying off in Italian lire rather than French francs."

Elaine reached for the telephone. Miracle of miracles, Luigi had the rooms. One more crisis had been met.

Just as Steve was leaving for lunch, the phone rang again. He stopped at the door and looked back.

Elaine answered it. She put a hand over the mouthpiece. "Mr. Kamiros."

Steve's face went expressionless. "Tell him I'll have his money for him Saturday morning." With that Steve turned and left. What was Conny trying to do, rub it in? Evidently, revenge was sweet to the Greek tycoon. Hell, Steve couldn't even remember the girl's name.

Ordinarily, he would have eaten at one of the hotels that housed his tourists, but somehow he wasn't up to the rich French cuisine. He drove back to the Pavilion Budapest, parked his car in the parking area and headed toward his trailer.

Carla called to him from the garden and he waved back. She said, "Did you see the Whiteley girl?"

He scowled and walked over to her. "Nadine? When?"

"Just now. She just drove into Monte Carlo to see you."

"I must have passed her on the road. Do you know what it was about?"

"Something about that man Silletoe. Steve, Carla thinks that man wants to marry her."

He cocked his head to one side questioningly. "Wants to marry you?"

"Don't be silly. He wants to marry Nadine. Nobody wants to marry Carla. She is much too old and...used."

"I'll marry you," Steve said, "just to keep you from continually carping about nobody wanting you. Sure Silletoe wants to marry her. She's got money."

The contessa nodded, worriedly. Uncharacteristically, she allowed Steve's gambit of humor to pass. She said, "But I am not sure that she has not accepted him."

"Don't be ridiculous."

The contessa shrugged.

Steve started for the trailer again. "I'll see her this afternoon."

He opened a can of mushroom soup, mixed it with milk from the refrigerator and put it on the buta gas stove. While it heated, he brought out English milk crackers, butter and a small wedge of Brie.

Confound Carla, she must be off her rocker. Particularly after that cable from her plant manager, Nadine couldn't possibly consider marrying that half-baked gangster.

Or could she? The girl was obviously so mixed up that almost anybody could sway her, given some sort of hold on her. What was it that Silletoe thought he had that would influence her decisions? He was sorry he'd missed the girl and wondered where she was now. Elaine would be able to tell her that he'd returned here.

He ate the soup, half a dozen of the crackers and the cheese, washed the dishes quickly, put away the balance of the food and then stripped for a quick swim. There wasn't any question of getting back to the office. Elaine could take over for the rest of the afternoon. Thursday afternoon was the nearest thing he had in the way of a day off during the height of the tourist season. At least, every other Thursday was. Elaine took it off one week, he the next.

He was irritated to see that someone else was on the beach. He hoped it wouldn't be one of his clients to whom he'd have to be polite and carry on a conversation.

It wasn't. It was Fay Gunther and she was breath-taking in a bikini composed of two wisps of textile and a prayer to keep them adhered to her lush body.

They stood and confronted each other for a moment. Steve didn't know what to make of her being here.

She raised highly plucked eyebrows questioningly. "You don't seem very glad to see me, Steven. I've been waiting for you for over an hour. The maid up at the house said you usually found time for a swim this afternoon."

"I was just surprised. Where's Mart?"

She sank down onto the sand. "Gone into Marseille to take care of the paper work involved in your business transaction. He won't be back until tomorrow." She peeked at him sideways. "You're the one person I know here on the Riviera, so I thought that we might renew an old acquaintanceship."

Even while he was reacting to the provocation of her figure and the undertones of her voice, Steve speculated about her motivation. It could have nothing to do with his bowing out of Gunther & Cogswell since he'd already agreed to that. Perhaps it was, as she said, pure boredom. She knew nobody here and Mart was gone for the day.

He took a place beside her, encircled his knees with his arms and said, apropos of nothing, "It's been a long time, Fay."

The corners of her full mouth dropped, seemingly half in sadness, half in humor. "Have you missed me, Steven?"

What a thing to say, considering the circumstances. He played it straight. "Sometimes. At first, quite a bit."

She took a handful of sand and let it dribble slowly from her fist back to the beach. "Very romantic, your dashing off like this and becoming a—what do you call them?"

"You mean expatriate?"

"Is that like Hemingway and Scott Fitzgerald, back in the twenties? You know, the Lost Generation?"

Steve laughed. It struck him that Fay might be quite the acme in sexual attractiveness but she was on the naïve side beneath her veneer of sophistication. They had reversed positions in that respect during the past five years.

"I suppose so," he said. "It seems to me that every generation, this century, seems to manage to get lost. What do they call this current batch—the beatniks?"

She laughed, too, but it didn't quite come off. It occurred to Steve Cogswell that Fay had never been much for humor. Laughter from her lips always seemed to have an artificial quality. Life was too serious for Fay for laughter. "The beatniks are old-hat now," she said. "The newest generation thinks they're old fogies."

To make conversation, Steve said. "How are you and Mart getting along, Fay? No children?"

She shrugged shoulders that were too white as shoulders on the Riviera went. She could have used more exposure to the sun. "No children." She added, seemingly idly, "As as matter of fact, Mart and I have become…well, more philosophical about our love life as the years have gone by." She laughed with a trace of embarrassment, as though letting him in on a family secret since they were such close acquaintances. "And as Mart's tummy has grown."

"Oh?" Steve said. She had assumed a prone posture now which had a wanton quality. He could feel his throat thicken, as it always did when the animal urge of sex was beginning to grow upon him. There were times when the bikini was more provocative than complete nudity.

She closed her eyes and turned her face directly to the sun. "This is probably a terrible thing to say, especially to you, Steven, but I've sometimes wondered what would have happened if you hadn't—well, discovered Mart and me that day. Possibly it would have all blown over, in time. I don't mind confessing that he isn't quite the man I once thought."

There was a simmering within Steve, but he said nothing.

She opened her eyes wide enough to look at him through eyelashes, and there was a roguish twist to her lips. "Though, of course, you weren't exactly a Hercules in that department yourself—were you?"

Steve said, and his voice had gone husky, as it always went husky, "Let's go up to the trailer for a drink?"

"Why not? And I'd like to see your little—would you call it a home?"

"The nearest thing I've had to one for five years."

She came gracefully to her feet and started toward the parked house trailer. Now she looked over her shoulder at him. "You're not bitter after all these years, are you, Steven?"

He followed her, unable to refrain from watching the sway of her hips. "I don't know," he said truthfully.

Her next words couldn't have been more unexpected. She said, very low, "Still love me, Steven?"

Steve Cogswell couldn't think of an answer. They were at the trailer now and he opened the screen door for her and let her precede him inside.

"Why, how clever," she exclaimed. "You know, I've never been in one of these before. Why, you've got everything." She turned and faced him. "You didn't answer me, Steven."

He tried to keep it light. "Sometimes I think so, Fay."

Her control seemed to slip. Over her always beautiful and controlled face, slipped a mask of gross sensuality, almost wantonness. Her eyes drooped and she swayed toward him.

As he grasped her, the tiny bathing suit halter dropped away and she stood nude except for the wisp about her hips. Her breasts were slightly heavier than he remembered them, and the tips were brown now rather than pink.

Afterward he never remembered removing his own trunks, nor the second piece of her bikini. They had stumbled, without releasing each other, both breathing hard, through the tiny trailer kitchen and into the bedroom beyond.

Stretched out on the bed, Fay had moaned in the manner that came back to him now as though there had been no five years between. She moaned and demanded him, her body squirming on the whiteness of the bed's sheets. The Venetian blinds of the trailer's windows were down, to exclude the heat of the sun's rays, and the room was almost as dark as it would be at night.

She moaned for him, but five years had passed since Steve Cogswell had played at love with Fay Hanlon. Five years in which he had desperately tried to prove her charges against him a falsehood. Rushing through his mind, like the flickering of an early Chaplin movie, went the faces of Danish girls and Swedes, of a Polish refugee he'd met in Paris, and a Parisian girl he'd spent a night with in Madrid, the wife of a Turkish diplomat he'd had an explosive affair with in Torremolinos, and the many tourist beauties he'd bedded here on the Riviera.

Much had gone by since last he'd known Fay's body. His fingers touched her here and there. His lips artfully played with her mouth and throat and burgeoning breasts, stirring a tumult of sensation within her.

It occurred to him that in spite of her appetites and sensuality Fay had probably never been subjected to other than very basic love techniques.

He whispered, "Have you ever had anyone do this to you, Fay?"

"Oh, no…no, don't. Oh, Steven, don't do that. You're killing me."

He moved slowly, ever so slowly. A touch here. A tantalizing of zones of Eros there. A kiss. A nibble.

She didn't know which way to turn. It was excruciating.

Somehow, Steven Cogswell seemed to be out of himself and away from all this even as he practiced a hundred tricks of eroticism upon her highly sexed, all-demanding body. He seemed to be able to stand back and watch, even as he performed. His own body, after all this stimulation, required animal fulfillment, but not as Fay's did. He could, at the same time, remain mentally aloof.

He played upon her naked, writhing body as a musician plays an instrument. And the music he brought forth was symphonic to her, but little more than discordant clashing notes to him. Even as he deftly and deliberately lifted her to a dizzy peak of feeling, a contempt and disgust were growing within him. Not solely with her, but with himself and the role he was playing as well.

She fell asleep, instantly, upon completion, a sleep of total exhaustion, and Steve Cogswell got up from the bed and looked down at her.

Welling up from within him was the contempt that he had felt for all women, these past five years, after their surrender to him. Fay proved no different from all the rest.

But this was Fay! This was the reason for it all! All these years he had been telling himself that though he slept with other women, he was still, beneath it all, in love with Fay.

But now he could see what he had been blind to before. The grossness that had begun to become evident in her face. Too long had she allowed herself to be the product of her passions. Her hips—the hips he had been admiring only an hour before—he saw now were beginning to show the first signs of fat. Her breasts were overly heavy, her legs beginning to lose firmness through lack of exercise.

His mouth feeling thick with distaste, he dressed himself. He put on a pair of heavy Swiss hiking shoes. He wanted to get out of here, and to walk, and to think.

She still slept as he left the trailer and made his way to the main highway. There was a feeling of cleanness, somehow, within him. It was as though he had been scoured by some powerful detergent. He was free. Free, at last, of Fay and the neurosis within him that had been Fay-based.

He strode through Beaulieu and toward Monaco, enjoying the warmth of summer air, the incomparable Riviera scenery, the breath of cool moisture in the wind that breathed over the Mediterranean.

I feel like running along the road at as fast a clip as I could make it. No, I feel like dropping into one of the bars along here and buying everybody champagne. No, I don't. No alcohol. I don't need alcohol. I'd like to go into the Casino and drop every cent I have on one number. I feel lucky. I feel luckier than I've ever felt before.

He had to laugh aloud at himself. He might feel lucky, but he didn't have enough money on hand to do any gambling, though he might be hot as a rocket. Not that he cared about the money. Let Conny take over his trailer and car. It was no longer important. He'd make out. Either at this job or some other.

In fact, he was getting tired of babying tourists. He'd have to look around and get into something with more of a future. Perhaps with one of the American engineering firms opening offices in booming, rapidly industrializing Europe.

A horn honked behind him, and he stepped further to the side of the road. It honked again, and he turned impatiently.

Nadine Whiteley waved to him from her Simca. She was headed in the opposite direction, back toward the Pavilion Budapest.

He walked back to her, said something jokingly, but she was obviously upset. He slipped into the seat next to her, dropping his own thoughts for the while and brought his mind to her problems.

Steve said, "The contessa said you were looking for me, Nadine."

"Yes. Yes, I was but that was earlier."

"Something to do with Silletoe?"

She was shaking her head in distress. "I don't know why I bother you. It isn't your problem."

He tried to bring her out of her depression with a light touch. "As representative of Far Away Holidays, your problems are mine so long as you're on this package vacation." He looked at his watch. "And that lasts until tomorrow at eleven o'clock, when your plane takes off for London."

"Oh, don't laugh at me, Steve."

His voice turned serious and he put a hand over hers, where she gripped the steering wheel tightly. "I wouldn't laugh *at* you, Nadine, only with you. You're a special person in my books."

Suddenly, there parked on the Shoreline Corniche, halfway between Beaulieu and Monte Carlo, she poured it all out to him. With the exception of old Dr. Levine, he was the only person in her life to whom she had bared her past.

She told him of Uncle Nat, and the rape, and the suicide. Of Roger Stuart and the thing that had happened to break up their engagement. Of Jerry Silletoe and her infatuation with him, and how it had come to a tragic climax. Of her resolve to face reality and deliberately to seek a love affair on the Côte d'Azur. And when she got that far, she looked pleadingly at him and flushed in embarrassment.

"I see," he said slowly. "And you picked me to be your temporary lover."

"Don't be angry with me, Steve. I'm so confused. Sometimes I think I've spent the past ten years and more being confused."

"I wasn't angry. Flattered. You're an attractive woman, Nadine."

She told him the rest of it. The latest developments. Of Silletoe and the photographs he had managed to get. And of the threats he had made.

The muscles in Steve Cogswell's jaws worked.

She ended miserably, "Perhaps he's right. He's strong and ruthless. Perhaps that's exactly what I need. This confusion can't last forever. I tell you, Steve, I'll wind up in an institution. It's just too—"

"No!" he snapped. "Jerry Silletoe wouldn't answer anything. That's obvious. And the moment he'd milked your fortune away from you, you'd be dropped. Don't bother to think otherwise. Where were you to meet him today?"

"He was going to get airplane tickets and pick me up at the Pavilion this afternoon."

"And you didn't tell him anything to the contrary?"

"He…he dominates me, Steve. I'm so confused. I just don't seem to have a will of my own."

"Let's go back to the Pavilion and wait for him. Sooner or later we're going to have to have it out with Jerry Silletoe and it's a lovely day for having it out. Thus far, things are going fine with me."

She slid over in the seat and he walked around the car and got behind the wheel. He drove the Simca back to the parking lot of the contessa's villa.

* * * *

They didn't have to wait for Jerry Silletoe. As they got out of the car, he arose from a stone bench upon which he'd been seated in the gardens that bordered the parking area. It occurred to Steve Cogswell that this was probably where Silletoe had waited the other night before assaulting and robbing him.

Silletoe sauntered forward easily, in full possession of himself and undoubtedly of the opinion that he controlled the situation. He smiled at Nadine and said, "About ready, darling? We have two hours before the plane takes off."

Steve said, "She's not going, Silletoe."

Silletoe's hard eyes went to Steve's and he looked the other up and down in contemptuous amusement. "Who told you that you had an opinion coming, Buster?"

Very clearly the words of the Nazi paratrooper now employed as a houseman at the Casino came back to Steve Cogswell. *You are raised a gentleman. You do not understand fighting. I understand fighting, this enemy of yours understands fighting. There is no gentlemen when there is fighting. There is only destroy or be destroyed. Sometimes there is only kill or be killed.*

Steve said clearly, "She's not going, Silletoe. Not with you. Not today, or any day."

Silletoe grinned. Incongruously, it made the man's gross face take on a boyish quality. He looked down at the ring on the second finger of his right hand. "That cut of yours is just about healed up again, isn't it, Buster?" Suddenly he glided forward in attack.

To Steve Cogswell it seemed as though his metabolism instantly changed. He seemed to be moving in a slow-motion world. A slow-motion world in which he was the only living thing traveling at the old rate. Nadine Whiteley stood to one side, motionless, both hands to her mouth. Jerry Silletoe was advancing, slowly but in grim and savage determination.

There is no gentlemen when there is fighting. There is only destroy or be destroyed.

Steve Cogswell's right foot, heavily shod with the Swiss hiking boot, lashed out cruelly to crack against Jerry Silletoe's shinbone. Still moving, seemingly in slow motion, the other's mouth opened in a roar of pain and he began involuntarily to bend forward to grasp his leg.

Quickly, efficiently, Steve Cogswell clasped his hands into a double fist and brought them crashing upward under the other's chin. Silletoe's head snapped back and he reeled backward, his mouth already gushing blood.

But Georg Herzog had been correct. Jerry Silletoe was an old pro when it came to street fighting, when it came to goon squads on the waterfront, when it came to union busting, when it came to a professionally administered beating.

He was down, but up again on one knee. He spat out a tooth, grinned even in his pain, muttered something incoherent that ended in "Buster," and then came in again to the attack.

Steve's feeling of perfect timing, of moving more quickly than the other was still with him. Silletoe attacked, in fighting stance, but Steve Cogswell worked on instinct. Had he attempted to meet Silletoe on his own grounds, he would have lost. But he didn't.

It was somewhat the position a chess expert finds himself in when confronted by a tyro. The tyro fails to make the standard moves and throws the pro off his game by doing the unexpected.

Steve rushed forward to meet his opponent but at the last split second he turned sideways and brought the heavy, spiked boot up in a kick to the side that gave him triple the leverage of a simple kick forward. In this position, the boot crushed into the kneecap, and the crack of bone could be heard over the rattling of the gravel upon which they battled.

Jerry Silletoe made a low animal cry of pain and began to slump forward. Steve moved in closer, grasped the other man's hair in both hands and slammed his head down savagely even as he brought his knee up into the other's throat.

Air whooshed from Silletoe's lungs, and he collapsed to the ground, unconscious.

Steve shook his head. He couldn't remember the other touching him, even once, but his body ached in several places and the side of his neck burned as though from a glancing, skin-abrading blow. Nadine stood watching him in fascinated horror.

He growled to himself. The past two or three minutes must have been the most brutal sight to which she had ever been submitted. However, the paratrooper had been right and there was no expecting combat to be pretty.

He said to her now, "If I know Silletoe's type, he's got his most important property on him. He wouldn't trust it with anyone else."

Steve went down to his knees and began tearing at the other's clothing. The wallet came first but there was nothing in it beyond the usual papers and a couple of hundred dollars' worth of francs. He patted the other's pockets, but discovered nothing more than routine possessions.

Surprisingly, it was Nadine who came up with the answer. "A money belt," she whispered.

Steve unbuckled the unconscious man's belt, zipped down the fly and pulled his pants open, his shirt tail out. Yes, there it was. A heavy money belt. Steve whipped it off and unsnapped the several pouches. He came to his feet.

There were two negatives and Nadine had no need to hold them to the sun to know what they were. There was also a large sheaf of new francs, at least twenty-five thousand of them.

Steve looked at her. And she at him.

He said, "Let's go somewhere and have a drink. A celebration is in order."

She looked down at the unconscious man. "But...but how about Jerry?"

That proved too much. Steve broke into spontaneous laughter in spite of himself. He said, "Somehow, I can't work up much interest in Mr. Silletoe's problems. However, I'll give Carla a shout and she'll see that he's taken care of."

* * * *

They enjoyed a strange euphoria. It was as though floodgates of emotional tension had broken for both of them and the pressures had been relieved. They felt like teenagers on their first date. Everything that was said was amusing. Everything seen was charming. Everything tasted was delicious. It was not quite dark as yet, but there were stars in the skies.

They stopped in Beaulieu at La Réserve and Steve introduced her to the champagne cocktail, failing to explain its sneaky attributes. He quoted Art Buchwald, "I like champagne because it tastes like your foot's asleep," and she dissolved into laughter.

They left La Réserve and went on into Monaco and had more champagne at the Summer Sporting Club, and then to the cabaret at the Casino.

Somewhere along the line he gave her a thumbnail autobiography and they decided that he was going to have to leave the Riviera and the hedonistic life he'd been leading and get back into industrial engineering. She agreed, though, that it would be impossible to return to Gunther & Cogswell. He was well rid of Fay and Mart.

Somewhere along the line, she amplified her own biography, which she'd touched upon that afternoon while parked in the Simca. And they decided that the thing she must do was return to the States and take Dr. Levine's advice about seeking psychotherapy.

And then they decided that all this was much too serious, in view of the fact that they were celebrating his release from Fay and hers from Silletoe, so they moved on to the Empire Room of the Hôtel de Paris for more champagne, and then to Le Knickerbocker to dance.

Five years of heavy drinking had given Steve Cogswell a tolerance for alcohol that allowed the evening's hilarious sampling of champagne to leave him only slightly affected. But of a sudden it became obvious that dancing was no longer for Nadine.

"I feel bubbly," she giggled.

Steve looked at her. He cocked his head to one side and considered. Finally he said, "You look bubbly."

"Maybe I better go home, Stevie darling. The waiters are beginning to look bubbly too. Especially that nice, red-faced one."

"When that happens," he nodded sagely, "the only thing to do is go home and sleep it off."

"I hate to ruin the party, bubbly. I mean Stevie."

"That's okay," Steve said. "But don't call me Stevie. That's what Mart always called me and he's gone to fat these days."

"I'll call you darling," she said, "because I like you and you're so bubbly."

"That I am," Steve admitted. "Both bubbly and darling. Wait till I get the check."

"The waiters are bubbly, too," she giggled, "but not like you."

"Nobody is as bubbly as me," Steve said. "It runs in the family."

He paid the check and managed, without too much difficulty, to get her out to the Citroën. They should have come in the Simca convertible, he decided, as he drove back to the Pavilion Budapest. The rush of the night air might have revived her. As it was, Nadine sat beside him, her head on his shoulder, soundly asleep, and snoring a slight little snore that amused him. The fact of the matter was that he was a bit tight himself but not impossibly so. He still felt fine.

He parked the car in one of the contessa's garages, and tried to revive Nadine with gentle shake, without luck.

He grinned down at her. "You can use the relaxation," he told her, "after the emotional wringer you've been through."

He went around to her side of the car, opened the door and slipped one hand under her knees, the other behind her shoulders, and lifted her out. She seemed light and comfortable in his arms, and his hand under her thighs tingled with the warmth of the softness of her legs.

Let's see now, she had mentioned a couple of days ago that she was in a room that enabled her to look down upon the beach and see his trailer. The only room where that was possible would be Number Eight.

He carried her to the back entrance of the villa to avoid observation and then after managing to wrestle the door open, to the back stairs and up to the second floor.

The door to Number Eight was unlocked. There were no keys at the contessa's. He got her inside, and stretched her out on the bed.

He stood for a moment, hands on hips, and scowled down thoughtfully at her. "Well, I don't imagine you'd mind," he said softly. "I've seen you in your birthday suit before."

Working gently, he managed to slip her simple cotton sports dress over her head. Beneath, a concession to August heat, she wore nothing other than brassiere and panties, both silken. He considered for a moment, shrugged and lowered both straps down over her shoulders and arms.

When the brassiere dropped below her breasts, he whistled appreciatively, and tugged the garment around so that he could get at the clasp. The panties snapped at one side, rather than depending on elastic, and he tugged them off in their turn.

He pursed his lips and murmured, "Someday you're going to make your husband awfully happy." He went to the closet and located a nightgown and after a certain amount of further difficulty, got it onto her, and then put her under the covers.

He turned to go, beginning to feel the champagne creeping up on him, and desiring his own bed, but for some reason he looked out the window down to where his trailer was parked.

There was a light showing in it.

For a moment he stared, uncomprehending, then he understood. Fay was still there. She had awakened from her sleep of sex saturation and was now awaiting his return.

His revulsion for her spread over him. He couldn't bear the thought of even seeing Fay now. He couldn't bear the possibility of her touching him, trying to arouse him to further love play. And he knew that was why she had remained.

He shook his head. The champagne was really creeping up on him and after the excitement and action of the day, he was utterly fagged. He looked back at Nadine and came to a quick decision. He undressed, threw his clothes over a handy chair, and slipped into bed next to her.

Steve Cogswell was asleep in a matter of seconds, the smile of content on his face matched only by that of Nadine Whiteley.

CHAPTER EIGHT

Friday, August 12th

Nadine Whiteley drifted upward from asleep and into the half-land between sleep and wakening. Even in this dream world she had a feeling of contentment and lazy comfort. She sleepily wondered why. What had happened to all the problems which beset her?

What problems? She vaguely tried to orientate herself. Ah, yes, her trip to the Riviera in her deliberate attempt to find a lover. But that problem was still with her. She had been unable to carry through her plan. Now she remembered—half-remembered—she was going to take Dr. Levine's advice and go to a psychiatrist. Yes, she and Steve had decided that would be best.

And then Jerry Silletoe came back to her thoughts. Ah, yes, that was a reason for her to feel relief. That problem had been solved when she recovered the negatives. When Steve had recovered them for her.

And then, flooding back to her came the memory of the night before. The celebration and the champagne, and the fun and the laughter, and how, toward the end of the evening, everything had seemed so bubbly to her, so amusing.

She laughed, awoke completely, and opened her eyes.

There on the pillow next to her was the head of Steve Cogswell.

Her eyes circled. For a split moment, there was panic in her, but then it was gone and nothing remained but shocked surprise. Frantically, she cast her memory backward.

It went no further than that night club. What was its name—Le Knickerbocker? They had gone there to dance but she had taken too much champagne. She vaguely remembered Steve getting her out to the car, and her calling him darling. And that was all.

And now here she was in bed with him, the morning's light

streaming in upon both of them. She had never been in bed with a man before. And now—Steve lay there, a smile of contentment on his face.

It was unbelievable.

But...but...shouldn't she feel something? Feel different? Possibly more *adult*, or *mature*, or something? She didn't feel any different at all, but, of course, that meant nothing.

Steve's own eyes opened and he looked at her, puzzled for a moment. Then he remembered.

"Morning, honey bun," he said sleepily. "Christ, we really hung one on, didn't we?" Then he realized she was bug-eying him as though he were a king cobra about to strike.

He began to explain, then pulled himself up short. He looked at her narrowly. Finally he said, his voice soft, "What's the matter, darling? Regrets, this morning?"

"Regrets?" She almost choked on the word.

He reached his hand out for his clothes, fished a package of Gauloises from a shirt pocket, located his matches and then punched his pillow hard and sat up in the bed, yawning. He lit the cigarette, drew smoke deep into his lungs and grinned at her.

She blinked, taking in his bare chest. She said, "I..." then stopped.

He grinned again and said, "Darling, you were wonderful."

The flush slowly rose from her neck to suffuse her face. "I...I was?" she said unbelievingly.

He nodded. "Wonderful. And you liked it, too, didn't you? I could tell."

"I *did?*"

"Well," he murmured with masculine superiority, "there's nothing like champagne to loosen up the libido."

She relaxed on her pillow, closed her eyes. "Good heavens," she said.

"What's the matter?" he said to her. He watched her narrowly.

"Nothing," she said finally. "Nothing is the matter, Steve. Everything has worked out. Everything is solved."

"You're wonderful," he said. "Come here, Nadine."

Her eyes shot open again, round as before. He put away his cigarette and turned to her.

She stuttered, "Again? In the morning, like this?" Her tongue moistened her lips.

"Why not?"

"I—why, I don't know. I just thought—well, isn't that something you do at night?"

His laugh was friendly and soothing, and he reached out and stroked her hair, spilling out as it was over the pillow's whiteness. "It's something you do any time when you're in love, honey bun."

All of a sudden, everything seemed to fit together for her. She was in his arms and she was saying, "Do you mean that really? Are you really in love with me?"

"Uh-huh, really."

"And...and am I in love with you?"

"Well, you certainly acted like it last night," he lied easily.

"I suppose I am, Steve. Oh, darling, I do love you."

He had cupped one of her rounded breasts in his right hand. Now he worked his fingers over it ever so gently until he could feel the nipple harden. She sighed, closed her eyes and relaxed.

She felt the fires commence to burn in her again as he began to play on her ready senses—at first subtly, compassionately, then with increased urgency as his own fires rose with their own savage demands.

With his hands, his lips, and finally with every taut muscle of his quivering body, he caressed her stiff-nippled breasts, the pulsing softness of her belly, the satin smoothness of her thighs—holding back nothing, yet never forcing her to take more than she was ready for....

Until, in full arousal, she began to moan incoherently and to drive her burning body against his, and he knew that this time she was really ready.

In the extremity of her need she seemed to writhe in almost semiconscious delirium as he lowered himself upon her. For one panicky instant he felt her go rigid as tender flesh merged with tender flesh.... Then, as his arms enfolded her in total, protective warmth, and her body closed finally around his, it was as though a dam inside her had broken open, and she was flooded with wave after wave of sensation, dizzying, all-consuming.

Now his carefully controlled movements brought her pulsing rhythm into exact harmony with his, and she found herself climbing, from height to height of unbelievable joy, toward a blinding pitch of awareness—until the fire which drove them both, almost unendurably, exploded over them in a sunburst of glory.

Afterward she lay back, almost in half-sleep again.

"It *is* wonderful, isn't it, Steve?"

He was up on one elbow, looking down at her, and now it was his turn for amazement. For the first time in more than five years, he realized, he had bedded a woman and then, afterward, felt only affection and tenderness toward her.

More than one trauma had ended in this bed, this morning.

She said sleepily, "Darling, when are we going to be married?"

Surprise upon surprise. He groped for his cigarettes, realizing that the idea appealed to him overwhelmingly. Two days ago had anyone suggested that he might one day remarry, he wouldn't even have bothered to laugh.

He lit up and said thoughtfully, "As soon as I can get reorganized, sweetheart."

"Reorganized?" She opened her eyes.

He said, reasonably, "I've got to get out of this job and back into my own field. All of a sudden, this life I've been leading nauseates me. I'll have to get back to the States, possibly take a few refresher courses, then get a job."

"But…that might take years."

"I can't see any alternative. But it shouldn't take that long."

"But, Steve, I own a whole town. A factory, all the houses, every store, every service station. Everything but the post office, which belongs to Uncle Sam." She laughed happily. "Don't you see? We'll have everything, even during the time you're getting readjusted. For that matter, why not take over management of the furniture factory? There's nothing to—"

"No," he said flatly.

"But Steve—"

His voice was emphatic. "I've spent five years associating with gigolos and the type of women who marry them, Nadine. I'm not going to become one. I'll come to you when I'm successful."

She said in irritation, "That's ridiculous. We both know you're no gigolo."

He climbed from the bed, began getting his clothes together.

"Where are you going?" she wailed, in alarm.

"I'm a working man," he explained. "This is Friday, my busiest day. I've got to get the old bunch of tourists off back to London, and greet the new batch, incoming at eleven o'clock."

"But *today*, of all days?"

He was slightly impatient with her. "A job's a job, Nadine. Somebody has to do it. You've got to remember that most people aren't born with money and consequently have to hold down jobs."

"That was a nasty thing to say."

"Sorry, but nevertheless I've got to start things rolling."

Her lips tightened in chagrin and she came out of the bed on her own side. "I suppose I'm one of your tourists that has to be put on the plane back to London, too. I suppose this sort of thing happens to you every week."

He took time out to look at her in exasperation. "Don't be ridiculous, honey. I just finished telling you that I loved you and want to marry you."

"You just finished telling me you wouldn't marry me. I'm beginning to suspect that this was just one more roll in the hay for you."

* * * *

There had been no time for reconciliation. They had remained in bed so late that Steve had time only to get dressed and up to Monaco to organize the gathering of the Far Away Holidays clients and make arrangements to get them to the airport on time.

He had hoped that Nadine would reconsider, get over her pique and remain at the Pavilion Budapest at least long enough for them to discuss future plans. It hadn't worked out that way.

When he got back from Monaco in the station wagon to pick up those clients who had spent the week at the contessa's villa, Nadine Whiteley wasn't among them.

He said to Carla, who was on the front veranda saying goodbys, "Where's Miss Whiteley?"

Carla said, "She took a cab to the airport. Said something about your station wagon being too crowded with so many." She added, "Carla thinks you have had a quarrel with Nadine."

"Well, Carla's right," Steve grumbled.

The contessa said carefully, "Women in love are not always so rational, Steve. Particularly if you are a woman who has gone for many years without love."

Steve said, "How did you know?"

She twisted her shoulders, characteristically. "Carla is a woman, too." She added with a return to her pixie quality, "And perhaps I have gone too long without love also, no?"

"But on the other hand, you're not irrational," Steve said. "Thanks, Carla. I'm trying to do what I can."

But there evidently was nothing that he could do. Carla had been right. A woman frustrated in love for as long as Nadine had been was not apt to be adjusted at this stage.

He argued with her at the airport, when he could find a few moments off from the demands of his one batch of tourists who were leaving, and the new batch coming in, but it did no good. She simply couldn't believe that if Steve loved her he wouldn't throw his job up and return immediately with her to the States to take a position at her furniture plant and live happily ever after.

He watched her plane take off bitterly.

* * * *

Steve had forgotten Fay Gunther. Forgotten her completely. When he entered his trailer he found her curled up on the couch reading an Olympia Press book. She had evidently not left the place since the day before. He could see dirty dishes and opened cans in the small kitchen that lay between living room and bedroom. The years hadn't changed Fay when it came to housecleaning, he noted glumly.

He was in no mood for her.

"Darling," she gushed. "I've waited for you."

"So I see. In this country, you'll have ants in that open food in a matter of hours."

"Ants! What difference does that make?"

"I live in this trailer," he said grimly.

She laughed. "Not any more," she said.

"Oh?" He put his hands on his hips and looked down at her. It was inconceivable to him that he could ever have loved this woman. Certainly inconceivable that he could have thought he did after what she had done to him and after five years.

Fay said, happily, "I've figured it all out while you were gone, darling." Her eyes narrowed. "By the way, we'll go into where you've been, later on."

She was being possessive yet! he told himself sourly.

She said, "We'll go back to New York and either you'll buy Mart out, or he can buy you out. And you'll go back into business."

"Using what for money?" Steve demanded, looking down at her wonderingly.

"Darling, you weren't taken in by Mart's story, were you? Why, Gunther & Cogswell is rolling in money. Simply rolling."

There was a quick knot in his stomach, but he said, "I rather figured out that things were going a little better than he said, but even so I haven't participated in the work for five years. I don't exactly bleed for Mart, but I haven't it in me to take him for the product of his work."

She laughed scornfully. "Product of his work! Why, everything that's developed since you left was the result of the outlines and plans you'd figured out for outfits like the Hammett chain in New England. You hadn't been gone a week before they signed up, and as a result of that success, the other papers you'd done layouts for signed up, too. The firm is riding high now, with a dozen employees and more assignments than it can handle."

"I see," Steve said.

"So there you are." Fay tossed her hands up happily. "I admit I was wrong, Steven. Completely wrong. You were the right man for me, all along. I just didn't know it." She looked at him archly. "You'll admit, until yesterday you hadn't let me know about your potentialities."

He said without bothering to attempt kindness, "No, Fay. I have no feeling for you whatsoever."

He couldn't have been more emphatic had he slapped her face. She said, "But yesterday…you *proved* you loved me."

"I'm afraid that doesn't come under the heading of love," he said. "It's no dice, Fay."

For the second time in his life, he saw the self-possession that was usually Fay Hanlon's dissolve into a shrieking, shrilling, hating, madwoman. The filth and obscenities flowed in an endless, breathless continuity from the white gash of her mouth.

Steve watched her a moment, wonderingly, unaffected and above it all. He wondered what kind of hell Mart Gunther had been through the past five years. Not that he cared.

He turned finally and left the trailer.

Steve Cogswell checked his wristwatch, then got back into the Citroën and drove to Nice and the Negresco Hotel. Mart Gunther hadn't returned from Marseille, so Steve phoned Elaine, in Monaco, and gave her some routine instructions.

He sat in the lobby, smoking quietly, thinking things out.

When Mart Gunther entered, Steve called to him. The heavy-set man came over, a grin on his lardy face. "All set, Stevie," he said. "I've got the papers and the five thousand. All I need is your signature, and the money is yours."

Steve didn't waste time on preliminaries. He said, flatly, "Fay told me the real worth of the firm, Mart."

The other's jaw dropped.

Steve pressed on. "I'm still willing to sell my half of the partnership, but not for five thousand."

It had come too quickly for Mart Gunther to adjust to the situation. He sputtered now, "You named the figure yourself. You said five thousand. A deal is a deal."

Steve didn't even bother to smile. He shook his head. "Don't be a fool, Mart. You were trying to cheat me. It didn't work. What I'll do is sell out to you for one-third of the real value of the firm."

Mart still tried. "I'd say that *was* about five thousand."

"Not from what Fay says, Mart. Just guessing, I'd say Gunther & Cogswell is pushing the million mark. At any rate, we can hire lawyers to take care of such details. My interest is getting out and the quicker the better. I'm demanding only one-third, rather than a full half because, admittedly, I've been out of it for the past five years. But give me any argument and I can get tougher in my stand."

Mart Gunther's plump lower lip went out in a pout, but he wasn't stupid and knew when he'd had it. "I'll kill that bitch," he muttered.

Steve nodded pleasantly, "Good idea," he said.

Mart snapped. "All right, it's a deal. Can you come back to the States immediately and work out the details with me?"

"I've got some things to wind up over here, but I'll locate some lawyers to meet with yours. Meanwhile, goodby, Mart. I hope we never have to see each other again." He turned to go.

"Wait a minute," Gunther said. "Where's Fay?"

"I neither know nor care," Steve told him, and was gone.

He drove the Citroën back to Monaco, checking his wristwatch again as he went. At the office, Elaine looked up wearily from her desk, Friday was always a hassle.

Steve said, "Congratulations."

She tried to think of some answer to that, and gave up, and waited for more developments.

He gave them to her. "Unless I'm badly mistaken, you are

about to become Far Away Holidays' representative on the Côte d'Azur. Get me the office up in London and Mr. Brett-James in person. I want to tender my resignation and, at the same time, recommend you for the job."

She was taken aback, but she reached for the phone. *"Oui, Monsieur Cogswell."*

"And speak English. You need the practice."

"Mais oui, Monsieur Cogswell."

He checked his watch again. He had to time this just right.

He gave his regrets to John Brett-James and gave Elaine Marimbert a big build-up, she'd been on the job for three years and knew it as well as he did himself. The boss sputtered a bit, then surrendered. He had no alternative.

Steve Cogswell put the phone down and pursed his lips in thought. He brought forth his wallet and counted out twenty-five thousand francs from the amount he'd rescued from Silletoe. Which reminded him to wonder what had happened to Silletoe; he had forgotten to ask Carla. The grifter had probably simply left town, once he'd recovered.

"Elaine," he said, "do one last chore for me, will you?"

"Enchanté, Monsieur Cogswell."

He grinned at her. "You're going to have to get over the habit of lapsing into French every time you become excited. On this job crises come up every day. Look, take this money over to Constantine Kamiros' office and give it to either him or Mr. Lindos, will you?"

She made a *moue*. "I forgot to tell you. When Mr. Kamiros phoned yesterday, he told me to tell you to forget about the money. He said—"

Steve shook his head. "Good old Conny. I might have known he wouldn't be able to stick it out. But take this over to him anyway." He checked his watch again.

When Elaine was gone, he sat down at the desk and brought the phone toward him. "If I know those Viscounts, that plane is pulling in right now," he muttered.

He called London Airport Central, proclaimed an emergency, and had them put Nadine Whiteley's name on the loudspeaker system.

In the background he could hear the announcement in heavy English accent. *"Nadine Whiteley. British United Airlines flight from Nice. Wanted on the telephone."* And over and over again.

Finally her voice came, breathless and puzzled. "This is Nadine Whiteley," she said.

"And this is your fiancé," he said. "Name of Steven Philip Cogswell. Now listen here. You get a room at the Savoy and don't stir out of it until I get there. I think I can get a night plane."

"Oh, Steve!" Her voice flooded with relief. "I was afraid I'd lost you. The minute the plane took off, I knew what a silly little fool I'd been—throwing away the one thing I went to the Riviera to find." Her voice broke. "Darling, you were so right. I don't want to marry a gigolo. And if you want your own business—"

"That's what I want," he said firmly. "Do you really see it my way—or are you just playing a conniving woman's game?"

"I've had my own way too long," she said softly. "And I'm not a conniving woman. Until I met you I was just a spoiled, love-starved New England-type virgin. From here on, I want everything *your* way."

"Well, then." Steve smiled to himself. "This is what I had in mind. I've come into some money since you left and my present plans involve, first, getting up there to London and marrying the girl I love and having a short honeymoon. Then returning here and winding up a few matters and then going home to the States and setting up in the industrial engineering dodge. How does that sound to you?"

"It sounds like the man I'm going to marry," she breathed.

"Just one more thing I like my way—the way it was last night and this morning." He paused, chuckling at her embarrassment at the other end of the wire. "And the minute I get into that room tonight—"

"Steve, please!" she protested, giggling. "Not on the telephone!"

But that didn't stop him.

ABOUT THE AUTHOR

Dallas McCord ('Mack') Reynolds was born in California in 1917. His father was the Socialist Labor Party Presidential Candidate on two occasions, and Reynolds' life an work were deeply affected by his political upbringing. After early careers in newspapers and computing, Reynolds returned from the Second World War and began to write science fiction. Based in Mexico but travelling widely in his role as Travel Editor for a men's magazine, he started slowly but surely to sell his work. Mack Reynolds wrote the first *Star Trek* novel, *Mission to Horatius*, and was once voted Most popular Science Fiction Author by the readers of *Galaxy Science Fiction* magazine. He died in 1983.

www.ingramcontent.com/pod-product-compliance
Lightning Source LLC
Chambersburg PA
CBHW030636130626
46552CB00002B/871